Elizab

MW01674558

Travels and Adventures of an Officer's Wife in India, China, and New Zealand

Vol. 1

SALZWASSER
VERLAG

Elizabeth M. Muter

Travels and Adventures of an Officer's Wife in India, China, and New Zealand

Vol. 1

Reprint of the original, first published in 1864.

1st Edition 2022 | ISBN: 978-3-75259-542-0

Verlag (Publisher): Salzwasser Verlag GmbH, Zeilweg 44, 60439 Frankfurt, Deutschland
Vertretungsberechtigt (Authorized to represent): E. Roepke, Zeilweg 44, 60439 Frankfurt, Deutschland
Druck (Print): Books on Demand GmbH, In de Tarpen 42, 22848 Norderstedt, Deutschland

TRAVELS AND ADVENTURES

IN

INDIA, CHINA, AND NEW ZEALAND.

TRAVELS AND ADVENTURES

OF

AN OFFICER'S WIFE

IN

INDIA, CHINA, AND NEW ZEALAND.

BY

MRS. MUTER.

IN TWO VOLUMES.

VOL. I.

LONDON:

1864.

PREFACE.

THE composition of this book occupied a voyage from China to England. Notes from my journal furnished the matter, my husband dictating while I wrote. Thus the contents came to be coloured by the peculiar character of his mind, and this preface was rendered necessary; for I cannot allow the work to go forth without this explanation. Professional subjects are touched on, which many of my readers will see could not have emanated from me. Lieutenant-Colonel Douglas Muter used the opportunity of stating opinions he strongly held, and which he thought might be useful; but he would be sorry they should be published under the shelter of a lady's name.

The original MS. was rambling and diffuse, having been commenced in the middle, and continued towards either end. Indeed it was in a very crude and incomplete state on our arrival in England. During our voyage to New Zealand it assumed its present form; and the chapters on that colony were added on the way from Dunedin to Calcutta.

At first the work was a subject of amusement, and furnished pleasant occupation for our time at sea. It was not, however, till it assumed some shape and consistency, that I entertained even the idea of publishing it; though my friends urged me to do so, on the plea that I had ample material, and that the adventures would be of interest to my countrywomen, as they portrayed the experiences of an officer's wife in the various countries visited by her.

CONTENTS

OF

THE FIRST VOLUME.

CHAPTER I.

Infantry Barracks at Meerut—Outbreak of Native Troops—I take Refuge at the Quarter Guard—Morning after the Mutiny—The Cantonment—The 60th Rifles paraded for Church—Military Proceedings against the Rebels—Conduct of the Sepoys—Incendiarism and Slaughter—Designs of the Mutineers—False Confidence in Native Troops—Their value overrated 1

CHAPTER II.

Feelings of the European Community after the Outbreak—Perils of Exposure to the Climate—Could Better Arrangements have been made for quelling the Mutiny?—British Residents at Meerut take Refuge in the Infantry and Artillery Lines—The Surrounding Country at Night—Murder and Pillage—Terrible Rumours—Fugitives from Delhi—Orders of the Commander-in-Chief—Martial Law Proclaimed—Punishment—British Force engaged with Mutineers—English Officers Killed 25

CHAPTER III.

Expected Attack on Meerut—Defensive Preparations—Warlike Rumours—My Khansumah and Ayah—Native Servants—Nunkin India—Beneficial Use of the Seventy-ninth Psalm—Massacre at Cawnpore—Effects of the Mutiny—Siege of Delhi—English Prestige—News of the Capture of Delhi reaches Meerut 41

CHAPTER IV.

Military Arrangements after the Fall of Delhi—Appearance of the City—The Palace—Fountains—The Peacock Throne—Scene of the Struggle—House of Sir Theophilus Metcalfe—The Cashmere Gate—The Chandnee Chowk—Effects of the War . . . 56

CHAPTER V.

Our Residence in the Captured City—Provisions—The English Mail—Want of Enterprise of the Gwalior Contingent—Search for Treasure—Concealment—Thirteen Waggons laden with Spoil—Jewelry and Precious Stones Captured—Miniatures—The Great Mogul a Prisoner—His Family—Commission for the Trial of Native Prisoners of Rank—Their Fate—Major Hodson—Conduct of the Royal Captives—The Jumma Musjid . 77

CHAPTER VI.

Return to Meerut—Convalescent Depôts—Entrance into Rohilcund of the Roorkee Field Force—The Base of the Himalayas enclosed by the Ganges—General Jones's Force—Crossing the Ford—Mistakes of the Sepoys—They are attacked by the Advancing Column in the Centre of the Terai—Flight of the Nawab—Attack on the Enemy's Position before Mooradabad, and their Defeat—Khan Bahadour Khan—Relief of Shahjehanpore—Sir Colin Campbell—Tremendous Heat 97

CHAPTER VII.

Tragedies at Shahjehanpore—Indian Travelling in Hot Weather—Intermittent Fever—Rewarding on Compulsion—Valour of the Seikhs—Entrance into the Punjab—Region of Hills—A Change for the Better . . 114

CHAPTER VIII.

A Bungalow in the Hills—Sanatorium at Murree—Firing Cannon at a Target—Mountainous Scenery—Military Command of the Station—Expensive Necessaries—Effects of a Damp Cloud—Attack of Malignant Cholera—Sir John Lawrence endeavours to check the Pestilence—Value of Sanatoriums—Attempts at Amusement—Winter on the Mountains—Last Days at Murree . . 124

CHAPTER IX.

Proceedings against the Mutineers at the Cantonment of Jhelum—A Comfortable House—Visit to the Fort of Moultan—Designs of the Mutineers—Their Excesses—Embark on Board the Steamer *Havelock*—The Indian Navy—Delicate Fish—Arrival at Kurrachee—The Cantonments 142

CHAPTER X.

On Board the *Eastern Monarch* bound for England—St. Helena and Longwood—Betting—Care of the Indian

Government for its Invalided Soldiers—The *Eastern Monarch* in the Channel—Steering for Portsmouth—The Ship on Fire and Laden with Saltpetre—Terrible Scenes—My Escape—Dreadful Conflagration—The Soldiers Saved—The Ship totally destroyed—My Arrival at Portsmouth—Reach London in the Race Week, without Luggage of any kind 160

CHAPTER XI.

Embarkation at Liverpool for Canada—The *Anglo-Saxon* and her Passengers—Fogs off Newfoundland—Icebergs—Quebec and its Scenery—Disappointment—Falls of Montmorenci—Citadel of Quebec and its Garrison—Steaming to Montreal—Yankee Barber—Kingstown—Arrival at Toronto—Opening of the University—State of the Country—Niagara Falls Station—Blondin and the Great Cataract—Primeval Forest 183

CHAPTER XII.

Grand Trunk Railway—Impressions of Canada—Return to England—The English Eleven, and the Yankee Twenty-two—Chinese Expedition—On board the *White Star*—Off Ireland—The Surgeon-Major and his School—Eclipse of the Sun—Good Ships in a Storm—Moon Blindness—Visit to Anjer—Dutch Formality—Pulo Sapeta . 212

CHAPTER XIII.

Chinese Junks—A Celestial Pilot—Pigeon English—Approach to Hong-Kong—Its Harbour and Shipping—Doctors' Shops—Sampans—Chinese Females—A Marine Portrait Painter—Cooking—Victoria Peak—Character of Hong-Kong 233

CHAPTER XIV.

A Collision in the Harbour—Voyage to the Gulf of Peiho—Difficulties of the Navigation—The Anchorage—A Gale—Perils of Disembarkation—Chinese Defences—Metamorphosed English Soldiers—River blocked up by Ice—Ineffectual Attempts to land—Disappointments—The Meatan Islands—Dangers of the Chinese Coast . 250

CHAPTER XV.

Transport of Troops—Accommodation in Ships selected—Objections to the Admiralty Scheme—Provisions and Liquor—Salt Food—Insufficient Rations for Soldiers on a Voyage—Captains of Transports—Mischief-Makers—Position of a Commanding Officer—The Queen's Regulations—A Dead Lock 265

CHAPTER XVI.

City of Victoria—Government House—Streets and Quays—The Queen's Road—General Hospital—Barracks—Jetty—Temporary Theatre—Chinese Shops and Merchandise—Quaint Sign-boards—Chinese Cruelty—Progress of Victoria—Medley of People and Confusion of Tongues — Buildings and House-rent—Graves — Unhealthiness of the Climate 285

CHAPTER XVII.

Annexation of Kowloon—Military Encampment—Hiring a Cook—Force of the Wind—Lawless People in Hong-Kong—Robberies and Assassinations—Catching a Tartar—Fireworks—Waste of Stores—Health of the Soldiers—A Country Recruit—Our Comprador . . . 304

TRAVELS AND ADVENTURES

IN

INDIA, CHINA, AND NEW ZEALAND.

CHAPTER I.

Infantry Barracks at Meerut—Outbreak of Native Troops—I take Refuge at the Quarter Guard—Morning after the Mutiny—The Cantonment—The 60th Rifles paraded for Church—Military Proceedings against the Rebels—Conduct of the Sepoys—Incendiarism and Slaughter—Designs of the Mutineers—False Confidence in Native Troops—Their value overrated.

ON Sunday, 10th May, 1857, I was at Meerut.

The 1st Battalion of the Royal Rifles, in which my husband was a Captain, occupied the Infantry Barracks. The men were parading for church, and Captain M. had left me to accompany them.

The sun was sinking in a blaze of fiery heat, that rose hazy and glowing from the baked plain.

I waited at the door of the church, expecting every moment to hear the sound of a gay march, which so strangely heralds the approach of a body of soldiers to Divine worship—but I listened in vain. A dull sound, very different from that I expected, came over the stillness of nature around like a distant waterfall; but I little heeded the holiday-making in the bazaars—holiday-making, as I then thought it, though it was the commencement of saturnalia destined to take a place in history, and to revolutionize the great empire which we had founded in the East.

A gentleman accosted me. "You need not wait, Mrs. M. Do not be alarmed, but an outbreak has taken place, requiring the presence of the troops, and there will be no service this evening."

The sun had set as I turned towards home, and was quickly followed by the dusk, which leaves so little space in this region between the glare of day and the darkness of night. I faced in the direction of the Native lines, and, in terror and amazement, beheld the horizon on fire, as if the whole cantonment were in flames. Entering the broad road that leads to the bazaar, I saw it was crowded with men.

Two of the European Artillery were hurrying up, pursued by a throng of natives hurling every missile they could get at the wounded and unarmed Englishmen. So intent were they on this occupation, that I was allowed to pass uninjured into a road leading to my home. The servants were assembled in a flutter of alarm, the Khansumah at their head. He declared he could not be responsible for any property, and bringing the silver in use he returned it to my charge. At the same time he advised me to conceal myself; a proposal which, from the indignant refusal on my face, he saw I regarded as an insult.

To conceal myself in my own home, in the lines held by a regiment that had reckoned up a century of renown! And from what? That was the question. Was the native army in revolt? Had the threatened storm come so soon, and was the instrument, so carefully sharpened by our Government, at its own throat?

The distant noise now rolled up, a Babel of voices nearly drowning the ceaseless rattle of musketry; and, above all, came the heavy tramp of an English battalion on the march, which can be distinguished at once from the movement of any other body by one accustomed to the sound.

The interview with my servants was interrupted by a sergeant sent by my husband, with directions for me to proceed to the Quarter Guard. He told me that the native force had broken into revolt, that they were shooting down every European they could meet, and that the English troops were moving on the bazaars. With drawn swords, the Chokedhar and the Khansumah escorted me to the place indicated, where I found many fugitives already assembled.

The scene at the Quarter Guard was not calculated to strengthen my fortitude. Fearful rumours were rapidly circulated, and as rapidly followed by others still more dreadful, and I was glad to accept a room close by, kindly offered to me by the wife of a pay-sergeant.

Every moment added to the noise; and through the roar of countless voices came the boom of heavy guns: one, two, three—then silence; and these dread messengers of good and evil tidings ceased for that night.

In the midst of the confusion a stranger presented himself with his family, directed by my husband to join me. His house, situated near the bazaar, had, with all its contents, been burnt to the ground, and the family had most narrowly escaped. The servants had concealed them under boughs of trees in the garden, from whence they witnessed the destruction of their property, and heard the savage demands made by the armed ruffians for the discovery of their retreat. When nearly every hope was gone, the place had been cleared by a party of the Rifles, and they were sent under escort to our house, whence they were directed to the Quarter Guard.

Before midnight the troops reached the Mall, where they bivouacked, throwing a chain of sentries around the European lines; and as I could then do so in safety, I returned to the house, accompanied by the fugitives.

All that night I walked in the verandah, watching the flames as they sprang up from the burning houses. I could see in the new fires the progress of the incendiaries, who sometimes approached, as I thought, perilously near our lines. The weary night ended, the last flames died out ere the rising sun reddened the sky, and I retired to rest with the impression of an event stamped on my mind that no time can erase.

The sun rose on a scene changed in a manner words cannot describe. It was not only that he had sunk on a peaceful parade for church, and rose on blackened ruins and murdered Christians; he had also sunk on good and kindly feelings, and now rose on the wildest storm of man's passions. It was mid-day turned to black night—a picture of peace changed by magic to one of war. We felt intuitively that it was a great revolution—a cyclone that had merely its centre at Meerut, destined to sweep, with a violence that would startle the world, over the length and the breadth of the land. Perhaps the framework of English rule would go down before the tempest, and if so, what fate was reserved for us?

I propose to give a slight sketch of the cantonment, that the event I have to record may be the better understood.

Meerut stands in the centre of the Doab, or territory between the rivers Ganges and Jumna. The country from the ranges of the Himalayah, for hundreds of miles towards Central India, is an unvaried plain. The station is one of the oldest in India, and in years gone by was held by a division of troops so large as almost to be termed an army. Then it was a frontier post, but as the frontier advanced, so advanced the troops, leaving behind vast ranges of barracks, rows of bungalows, shops, roads, trees, and all the civilization that time and a great expenditure can alone produce. The barracks of the English troops occupied a line of great extent, fronting a noble parade-ground cleared from every impediment to the movement of men. The head-quarters of the Bengal Artillery were on the right; the Rifles in the infantry barracks were in the centre; and the Sixth Dragoon Guards (Carabiniers) in the Cavalry barracks on the left.

The military stations in India are on the plan of a camp. The lines occupied by the men face to the clear and open country; next come the hospital, cook-houses, gymnasia, canteens, and other buildings; and then the houses of the officers. To the rear of these, in Meerut, ran a magnificent road termed the Mall, and behind that the space was filled up by numerous houses and bazaars. The only inclosed buildings were the Dum-Dum and the

General Hospital; the former behind the Artillery, containing stores for that branch of the service; and the latter in rear of the Infantry. A wide space separated the Artillery and Infantry from the Cavalry, who occupied a long range of handsome barracks just completed.

The Native lines faced to the left of those held by the English troops, commencing about a mile or so to their rear. They were very extensive, having been built for seven battalions. The long rows of bungalows for the officers of these battalions were separated from the chief, or Suddur, bazaar only by a street. I need scarcely add that each bungalow stands in a garden called a compound. This bazaar, in 1857, had more pretensions to be termed a city than many of the most populous towns of India.

If lines were drawn at right angles from the right of the European and from the left of the Native barracks to the rear, at the point where they met, the square would be complete; and all that space, containing many thousands of acres, was crowded with the residences of civil and military functionaries, citizens, public buildings, and bazaars. The whole was shaded by the foliage of well-grown trees, and intersected with numerous and beautifully constructed roads.

The walled city that gives its name to the station lies a short way behind the Suddur Bazaar.

The great cantonment was built with no more regard to defence than Cheltenham or Manchester. Our maxim was that we must beat our enemy in the open field, or wherever he might be entrenched, or cease to rule in India. Armies had gone forth from Meerut to conquer provinces—no one dreamt that the time would come when we should there tremble for our lives. One of the objects for which this spot was selected, was to overawe the Imperial city of Delhi, distant about thirty-five miles, by a good road. It was not imagined that the turn of events would reverse this order, and that the period would arrive when the Imperial city would overawe the military station.

The Rifles had assembled on the parade ground. The men were standing in groups, ready to fall in on the sound of the bugle, and the officers were scattered in little knots, when suddenly a stream of soldiers poured tumultuously towards their barrack-rooms.

"What is the matter?" was the general exclamation.

"The Sepoys are in mutiny!" was the answer.

Without orders the parade was changed. They had been waiting without arms for Divine service —they now came forth armed and accoutred for action. The convalescent, the excused, those going on pass—all rushed into the ranks; and the colonel, who attended to march the men to church, found the soldiers in column of *route*, ready to engage an enemy. Thus, the first move made in one of England's most momentous wars was by the private soldiers, who seemed to have a keen appreciation of the crisis and of the work before them. Ammunition was distributed, and a company was despatched to the Treasury. The Native guard, in charge of a Native officer, had turned out with their arms in their hands, and seemed irresolute as to their course, when this company came up at the double, and halted before them. The guard was disarmed, the records and treasure saved, and the incendiaries checked in that quarter.

All the guards, save those over the quarters of the European forces, are given by the Native Infantry. Even in the lines of regiments, Native sentries mount over the Quartermaster's stores. When the ammunition was sent for, the Native guard was seen sneaking away. So rapidly had the Sixtieth got under arms, that they could with ease have captured all the natives on duty in their lines, but neither the officers nor the men had a notion of the length to which the mutiny had proceeded, and they waited impatiently for orders to act.

In the meantime, the surprise was so complete, that the Chief Commissioner became aware of his danger only when men were yelling in tens of thousands around his house, and he was roused from his security to trust his own life and his wife's into the hands of his servants, who safely carried them through that night of danger. The General escaped by a back way, and the Brigadier rode at full speed from his home with the bullets of his own guard whistling past his head. Probably this officer, whose good fortune it was to strike the fatal blow at Delhi, never more nearly met his fate.

While the chiefs were concealing themselves, or riding for their lives, the bazaars were in the hands of myriads of Goojurs* and badhmashes,† who had assembled from the surrounding country to assist in the extermination of the English, and to sack the cantonment.

The Brigadier rode up, and the battalion moved at once on the bazaar. It was joined by a battery of artillery and some troops of cavalry. Fearing to entangle this small force among the dense masses that filled the streets, and a Native force stronger than his own, the General passed to the right and formed on the parade-ground in front of the Native lines.

The sun had set, and the moon had not yet lit up the scene. The illumination before him, rising out of the thick blackness around, was one of awful grandeur. For more than a mile three rows of thatched bungalows were on fire, and the spaces between seemed filled with a legion of fiends. As the skirmishers drew close, mounted Sowars with drawn sabres were seen riding furiously about in the light of the conflagration; but the troops approached in darkness, and it was not till the Enfield bullet, in its deadly flight, passed close by that the

* A plundering Gipsy tribe.

† Rogues and vagabonds in the city.

mutineers knew their danger. Drawing rapidly to their left, the loud hum told the Brigadier they were congregating on his right. Some guns were unlimbered, and the multitude was dispersed with three rounds of grape. This was the last ever seen of the Native army of Bengal in the lines of Meerut.

The troops passed through the bazaars, driving the Goojurs from the gardens of the houses. In the streets not a human being was to be seen, though half an hour before they were filled with the predatory tribes for which in former years this neighbourhood was notorious. A few mangled victims were taken from the ditches, and the force bivouacked on the Mall, throwing a chain of sentries around their lines. So continuous was the musketry in the bazaars, that it sounded as if a great action were going on; and amidst the cries of the frantic Goojurs, and the blaze of the houses in flames around, I venture to say that few slept that night within miles of the circle of Meerut.

The conduct of the Sepoys, in avoiding the battle here offered, damped the ardour of their Meerut partisans. They had boasted everywhere that they were more than a match for the European garrison; yet they fled, scarcely firing a shot not discharged at an unarmed man.

At dawn the Brigade again marched on the native lines, seeking out the enemy, whose course was not yet known; but at that time the Sowars were riding into the city of Delhi. Far over the clear and level parade-ground a crowd of Goojurs hung like a cloud, and a similar body could be traced during the day in the neighbourhood of the European lines. For some time these men waited the evacuation of Meerut, or the destruction of the English, for on this they seem with confidence to have calculated. They were soon to learn the nature of the champion they had backed, and that those who intend to prey on British spoil must act with courage, and nerve every sinew for the enterprise. From amidst the yet smoking ruins of the houses, from the streets, and from ditches, the remains of the murdered were taken; and with horror the officers saw the mangled bodies, scarcely to be distinguished, of ladies they knew well, lying naked in the street, and hacked with sabres. The soldiers picked up their comrades. The men spoke little—there was no outburst of feeling, though in their hearts was seared the memory of this scene.

Though I shrink from details, yet a sketch is necessary—for the horrible character of the outbreak is not fully understood in England. Frequently I have been asked if the reported murders and escapes were true, and even if any foundation existed for such reports! In the first instance, as usual, the nation exaggerated the crimes of the rebellion, and ended, in the reaction sure to follow, by disbelieving plain and true statements. To such a result tended the accounts of men who saw the retribution—but not the provocation; who beheld the cringing figure and clasped hands of the wretch mercilessly consigned to the gallows—but not the yelling fiend, with dripping sword and hands red with blood, mutilating the bodies of those who had never injured him.

I will take the first house, which became a true type of what numbers throughout India were destined to become; and one spot of road-side, which furnished but a poor sample of many more horrible scenes.

Near the gaol stood a neat brick chunammed bungalow. This gaol held the Sowars, whose sentence of imprisonment had precipitated the revolt. It was situated behind the lines of their corps, and the first act of the Third Cavalry, who led the outbreak, was to release their comrades and the other convicts in confinement.

It was Sunday evening, and I believe a few friends had assembled in this house. They must have been surrounded, and every hope of escape lost, before even a conception of what was impending had entered their minds.

The conclusions Captain M. formed were from what he saw. It seemed that they had fled to their bed and bath-rooms, seeking any hiding-place in their desperate extremity.

Attempts had been made to burn down the bungalow, which were defeated by the nature of its materials, and the volumes of smoke had only blackened the walls and the ceilings, as if to throw a pall over the tragic acts the fire refused to obliterate, leaving the place a charnel-house, black with crime. The doors and window-frames had been torn from their positions, the furniture was gone, the matting in shreds, and trampled by a thousand feet, the plaster soiled and broken.

Following in the flight of the inmates, a bedroom was entered, where a pile in the centre attracted attention, requiring an inspection to understand what it was. Charred ends of chairs and tables were mixed with burnt ends of limbs and fragments of garments! The proceedings, of which the proofs lay here, were difficult to realize, and took some time to comprehend. Men and women dying from sword cut wounds must have been heaped upon their own broken furniture, till the vestiges left by the fire applied to the pile did not even tell the number of the victims. The walls were dark with smoke—the floor stained with blood—and the air tainted with the smell. It was easy to trace the rush of desperate men into the small adjoining apartments, where their bodies lay just as they had furnished subjects for the brave swords of the rabble to hack at and to hew.

However sad may be the look of a soldier on the field after an action, there is no horror in the gaze on the dead who fell fairly with arms in their hands, and the excitement of battle in their hearts. But it shocks even the sternest to see men murdered by their bedsides, and still more to see women. Before the frenzy of excess that suggested and carried out the funeral pile, the soldier stood aghast; and an impression was produced perhaps never afterwards erased.

A little way from this spot two riflemen of my husband's company lay on the road, in such a state that none save their own comrades could recognize them. On the evening preceding the mutiny they had received an advance of pay with a furlough, and were bound to the hills in a government bullock van, when they were attacked by the mob, the first in this attack being their driver. The body of a lady lay in a ditch on the other side of a slight embankment, so disfigured by wounds as to be with difficulty recognised. A track was discernible along the duct of the road from the bazaar to the place, shewing clearly she had been dragged over the ground, and thrown where she lay. The corpse of another murdered woman was in the same ditch, a little beyond.

But why follow these details—why wonder that our country people cannot comprehend the full barbarity of these unprovoked massacres, when those who saw them recall the scenes more as a dream than as a reality—an enduring impression left by a hideous vision? This bazaar was only three or four hours in the hands of the mutineers; and as my mind wanders from cantonment to cantonment that fell wholly into their possession, a shifting scene of horror goes by, which I know only faintly portrays the facts.

It was probable that the mutiny would begin at a station held by European troops, from the fact that these only had the commanders who had the power to coerce; and so it proved, for it was in the attempt to punish the mutinous conduct of the 3rd Cavalry that the revolt was precipitated. How much we owe to this precipitation, may be best conjectured by considering the plan said to have been proposed by the Sepoys. On the Queen's birthday, which was to be celebrated one fortnight later, they were to parade, according to their plot, with arms loaded, and pouches filled with ball-cartridge. It was then the custom for British regiments to stand by the side of Indian battalions, and fire a *feu-de-joie* in honour of the event. The captain of each company of Europeans sees the service ammunition carefully removed, and its place supplied by three rounds of blank. While the English soldier was discharging his harmless powder in the air, the bullets of his Hindoo ally were to be directed at his heart.

The scheme was simple and practicable in the highest degree; and if carried out with secrecy and resolution, would have swept every European soldier, in one and the same hour, from the face of India. A massacre more foul—more wide-spread—more disastrous—had never before been so completely in the power of a people. Had it been carried out, Her Majesty would have had the heart-rending reflection that her birthday was the blackest in the annals of a nation whose history extends over a thousand years, and whose operations embrace the globe. If ever in human events the hand of God has been manifest, it was displayed during this perilous period. From the commencement of the outbreak to the fall of Delhi, our career was a succession of miraculous deliverances; and perhaps there was no officer of experience and intelligence in the country who would have considered our escape possible, in the event of a general mutiny of the Bengal army, had the opinion been asked before the mutiny began.

The General who commanded the Meerut division had been trained in a Native regiment. One of the points of such training was to place the utmost confidence in the valour and fidelity of the Sepoys. The officers boasted that these battalions had broken French regiments in fair and open fight, and had advanced in the face of dangers where even British troops had flinched. The effects of this teaching were seen when the mutiny commenced. The officers of the regiments which had not yet mutinied pledged their lives on the fidelity of their men, and many fell victims to the noble feeling of confidence nothing could shake. These officers, with the same confidence, would have led their men against any enemy. It was not fair to expect the General to act in direct contradiction to this feeling, so carefully fostered by the nation itself.

The Native garrison, consisting of the 11th and 20th Bengal Infantry, and the 3rd Cavalry, were about equal in numbers to the European soldiers. These men openly bragged of the courage for which they had been lauded in the despatches of a century, with all a Native's hectoring. The people around believed in them. They were aided by tens of thousands of Goojurs and of camp followers. The three regiments rose suddenly on the station, unprepared, with arms in their hands and ammunition in their pouches. The surprise is that so little, not that so much, was effected.

It is impossible to foretell what the result would have been had they marched immediately on the European lines, or even defended their own against our attack—as was done with so fatal an effect at Jhelum. The first course might have been destruction; the last must have been disastrous to us; for the Sepoys were in a position to bear a heavy loss, while each European soldier killed was a direct step towards their goal.

But could the bloodshed of the mutiny have been prevented by a close pursuit, and the revolt nipped in the bud?

The experiment might have been successful, but is far more likely to have led to the most disastrous consequences.

Nothing except the actual trial could have shown the Native army that the power to make or mar English rule in India was not in their hands. They held that the empire had been conquered for us by themselves; and persuaded they were the kingmakers, they naturally considered it wiser to transfer the rule to their own hands, than to allow it to remain in ours; and they believed the time had come for this transfer. People argue as if the Indian revolution was a mere accident, depending on local causes or an energetic general; while it was the sure effect of a chain of circumstances leading directly to such a result.

The mutiny at Vellore was a mere outbreak of fanaticism and folly—that at Meerut the beginning of a struggle for empire. Any serious check at the commencement would have been ruinous to us. Might not such a check have followed the dispatch of a few hundreds of men to a city filled with fanatics, and in the hands of a revolted garrison, consisting of regiments of all arms, complete in every appointment?

The officer who had first to test the real value of these regiments, where such great interests hung on the result, might well pause to gather around him every element of strength. Subsequent events showed that the Sepoy had been overrated—that he ceased to be formidable when deprived of his English officers. Without them he was a tiger with his teeth extracted and his claws pared; and no answer could be more complete than this to the abuse so often heaped on our military officers. The English officer has led the battalions of Portugal to beat those of France, and the hordes of Turkey to repulse the regiments of Russia; he has shed over this Hindoo army a century of renown; and in the most isolated positions, supported by courage and strength of character, he has bent and swayed the wild tribes around, directing by force of will their untrained energies and valour into channels useful to his country; but by far the greatest of his exploits has been the conquest and fame his leadership has extracted from materials so worthless as this Hindoo army.

I believe that the mutiny could not have been checked by the European garrison of Meerut, and that the immediate employment of this force in its suppression would have led to the most serious disasters.

CHAPTER II.

Feelings of the European Community after the Outbreak—Perils of Exposure to the Climate—Could Better Arrangements have been made for quelling the Mutiny?—British Residents at Meerut take Refuge in the Infantry and Artillery Lines—The Surrounding Country at Night—Murder and Pillage—Terrible Rumours—Fugitives from Delhi—Orders of the Commander-in-Chief—Martial Law Proclaimed—Punishment—British Force engaged with Mutineers—English Officers Killed.

THE first feeling at Meerut was akin to despair. The small body of British knew that they would be opposed to the whole Bengal army, in possession of immense magazines and stores; and from the savage manner the Goojurs, as well as camp followers, had handled the stragglers they met, the idea was that millions of Natives would be in insurrection around.

Those unacquainted with the climate of the North West Provinces in May and June can form no conception of the task that fell to our countrymen. It was supposed to be impossible for us during these months to exist under canvas; and this opinion was calculated on by the Sepoys when planning the outbreak. Stringent orders were in force against exposure from a short period after sunrise until sunset; but notwithstanding every care and excellent barrack accommodation, many annually died from excessive heat.

It was with no feelings of surprise that the tidings were received of the rise at Delhi, and the massacre of the Christian community. It will be an open question for history whether those massacres could have been prevented by any move of the Meerut garrison. The General and the Brigade were much blamed at the time; and I think with as much reason as a well-found ship struggling in a hurricane might be blamed for looking on at an ill-found vessel overwhelmed by the same blast, without making a useless as well as dangerous attempt to save the crew. If a march on the imperial city would have been a false move, endangering the empire, the Christian community could not thus have been saved. Even had that move been made, and been a success, it is doubtful whether it would have saved these people. All the arguments hinge on the supposition that the Native army would not have fought—a supposition in direct opposition to facts. For the same reason that the regiments at Meerut rose to save their comrades from imprisonment, the regiments at Delhi would rise to save them from the gallows.

It has often been said that the sight of a body of Dragoons crossing the bridge of boats would have changed the aspect of affairs, cowed the city, and quelled the mutinous spirit. It is a pity that the whole force of these Dragoons, backed by the Artillery and the Rifles—whose bullets afterwards told with such deadly effect—could not suppress the insurrection at the spot where it originated. This argument renders Euclid's axiom thus: "A part is greater than the whole;" and makes it, when so put, of double force, as the Sepoys at Delhi were increased three-fold, while our strength would have been diminished at least in that ratio, if we had despatched a force in pursuit—comparing the detachment with the Meerut garrison. I believe that the dust raised by the Dragoons would have been the signal for the massacre of every Christian in Delhi, and for a strife that might have ended in the massacre of every Christian in these provinces. And in this I am also borne out by the occurrences at Meerut. The Sepoys, the camp followers, the Goojurs, hastened to kill when they rose; and though the English garrison was only a mile distant, its people could not be saved, whom the mob had surrounded. With their fate before us, can it be supposed that the Christians entangled in the most fanatical city in India, encompassed by walls, could have been preserved by a portion of that garrison, thirty-five miles off, who had failed in this very object in their own cantonment?

If the insurgent Sepoys from Meerut had found the road barred, and had taken another direction, it is clear the English in Delhi would have been in a similar position as at Cawnpore, or at Bareilly, and perhaps even fewer might have eventually escaped. The intelligence of the rise at Meerut at once made mutineers of all Native garrisons.

The subsequent history of every one in Bengal, where no European troops were quartered, was the record of an attempt to avert or delay the catastrophe, ending in a ride for life, and a massacre. It cannot be supposed that this garrison would not be affected by the news, stationed as it was in the very focus whence the treason emanated. Sooner or later this portion of the Native soldiery was sure to rise; and the fanatical and disaffected citizens even more certain still,—whether or not a mutineer from Meerut had entered the capital of the emperor.

Within that fortified city was our greatest arsenal. Its name touches a chord in the Mussulman's heart, and its history gives to it a political importance which neither its wealth nor population warrants. It was natural that the mutiny should gather to a head in this strong city—strong in the moral power which the possession of the recognised capital of India gives—stronger still with the representative of the ancient emperors supporting the revolt from the seat where his ancestors had for centuries governed the empire, and stronger yet in all the materials of war.

As the Native regiments poured into Delhi, the British residents in Meerut left their houses and concentrated in the Infantry and Artillery lines, abandoning the barracks of the Cavalry; and thus the whole force was grouped within a small circle. The Dum-Dum and the General Hospital were fortified; *chevaux-de-frise* bristled in front, and from embrasures the mouths of cannon menaced the surrounding country.

Within the circle was full of life; officers and men lounged about, horses were picketed in long rows, guards held every post, sentries challenged in all directions, and gangs of Coolies were constantly at work.

Outside this busy ring, the country wore the most miserable aspect. The gardens around the desolate houses were hastening to decay; nothing stirred on the roads once so gay with life; here and there the blackened walls of a bungalow destroyed on the tenth stood drearily up; but the scene of the great ruin was in the Native lines. There streets of houses had been consumed, and it is impossible to convey a just idea of its sadness. The charred rafters, the black walls, the broken carriage resting on a half-burnt wheel, the skeleton of a bullock lying on a bed of withered flowers—dead, for want of the water it once drew; the blasted trees, scorched in the great fire—all combined, with the recollection of the fate of the inhabitants, to form a picture so painfully desolate that the spot was rarely visited.

The bazaars were silent, as if depopulated by a plague; scarcely a Native was to be seen. Trade had ceased; the telegraph wire lay cut on the ground, and the poles were rotting by its side—no means of communication existed. Even the peasant ceased to cultivate, and it became difficult to believe that the district was one of the best tilled and the most populous in the world.

At night all this was strangely changed. The ceaseless boom of powder ignited in chatties sounded like cannon from the surrounding villages; the horizon was lit up by great fires, and officers speculated, as they gazed at the glare of a distant flame, on what village or town was being destroyed. Without intermission the sound of musketry continued from the neighbouring bazaars, to warn off murderers and robbers who stalked abroad. Even within a short distance of our fortifications, a party who rode into a village found the inhabitants lying dead in the streets, and some women and children weeping over the bodies of their kindred.

So this province, that knew war only by tradition, or by the accounts of far-off battles—where even an execution was rare—became at once steeped in blood. Fire ran over the land—wholesale murder shocked mankind—and pillage and revenge took the place of law. It may be that the natural bent of the people, repressed by the hand of power, rebounded with violence when that pressure was removed. Men that could not be roused to patriotism rose to rapine—village wreaked its hoarded vengeance upon village—man on man. The cruel Asiatic, in his frenzy, spared neither women nor children; and when these were the wives and little ones of his Saxon ruler, he struck a blow that stirred the deep heart of that master.

How far the people were really hostile we could not then ascertain, but it was clear that there was a large element in the population that eagerly seized the opportunity to give scope to their lawless instincts.

Besides the families who had forsaken their houses, the refugees from the district assembled in the Dum-Dum, and the life it then presented was new to us all. The principal buildings were three long barracks, and the families were there grouped together during the day—the ladies at work and the children at play—eating at long tables, and living more in public than accords with

English tastes. Every available spot was covered with a tent, where the nights were passed; some held the guards of the Dum-Dum, and the wife of a judge and the soldier on duty were placed in close proximity.

Terrible stories circulated freely in these barrack-rooms, for the thoughts of all were centred in one great object, and the eager anxiety for news rose almost to a mania. Manufacturers of gup,* as it was termed, had a lively time, and imagination was freely called into play; yet imagination and fiction, with every advantage, were beaten by the truth, for I remember no story, however horrible, that equalled the realities of Cawnpore.

The first rumours related to the march of the Sappers from the engineer station of Roorkee, and that of Major Reid's regiment of Goorkhas from Deyhra Dhoon. Great doubts were expressed regarding the fidelity of the former. First, it was reported they had killed their officers and marched for Delhi; next, they were depicted as filled with horror at the conduct of the Cavalry and Infantry; but the strangest course was that which they actually took, for they marched into Meerut only to mur-

* Gossip.

der their commander, and many of them to fall under the sabres of the 6th Dragoon Guards. The true and gallant conduct of Major Reid's Goorkhas, which is now historical, was, even then, scarcely doubted.

Among the fugitives were many who had escaped from the massacre at Delhi. Tender women, who had sprung down the fortifications amid a storm of bullets—who had waded through rapid rivers, and walked under a sun whose scorching rays cannot be known save by those who have felt them—stealing along paths occupied by a hostile population. What heroism!—what endurance!—what hair-breadth escapes! These plain narratives contained examples to nerve men's hearts for the terrible strife before them, and, if needs be, to show us all how to die with fortitude.

The surgeon had given me a room in the Rifle hospital, until wanted for sick or wounded soldiers, and our servants and furniture were removed to this asylum. These buildings were not so extensively fortified as the Dum-Dum, but the rooms were filled with sick, who were armed, and, however ill, would turn out to fight, if the necessity arose. I was thankful for the security, as my husband was constantly engaged on duty—a third of the battalion being required each night to rest on their arms on the Mall. My life here was much more quiet than in the Dum-Dum, though it was less sustained by companionship and the exciting tales there constantly afloat.

The news of the mutiny spread through India like wild-fire, and reached the Commander-in-chief at Simla. Instantly the three regiments in the hills were ordered to Umballa, and the Delhi Field Force rapidly assembled there, under the personal command of his Excellency. For a brief period the communication with Agra, by telegraph, was restored, and the General received his instructions to detach a large portion of his force to join the Commander-in-chief, and to proclaim martial law in the district. Then the waves of the rebellion surged over the country, and left Meerut like a rock isolated in a sea of trouble.

However, martial law had already been proclaimed, and Meerut had tasted of the bitterness felt by the English, and infused into their acts by the proceedings I have described. A gallows had been erected not far from the burial-ground, where lay the victims of the Meerut massacre. The first to suffer was a butcher, who had taken the most active part in the murder of a lady; he had been captured gallantly by an officer, and was hanged by ordered of the General.

The most ferocious of the many who had assisted in the fire and bloodshed that had desolated the station were to be found among our own camp followers. The butchers led, and, it is said, the tailors strove to vie with them; then came masons, carpenters, bakers, and all the rabble who had rushed into the streets on that fatal evening to destroy the unarmed soldier whom fate had brought in their way in his afternoon stroll. The butchers followed the Sepoys to Delhi, and perhaps took part in the crimes there perpetrated.

When this engrossing pursuit ended, they returned to Meerut to resume their avocations, where they were seized and compelled to undergo an ordeal which blanched the cheeks and shook the limbs of many who had been loudest in cry and foremost in cruelty, and exposed them to each other as the cowardly ruffians they were. It was difficult to obtain evidence, and they were sent round the garrison, drawn up in a row; while company after company, and troop after troop, was halted before them, and the men asked if they could recognise any of the number as having been engaged in the riots. Most of their faces wore a deadly hue—some could scarcely stand, and all their lips muttered prayers, the name of Allah alone being distinguishable.

The Natives condemned to death generally assumed a stoical indifference, and moved with composure to the place of execution, sometimes picking their way over ground wet with heavy showers, as if more concerned for their health than for their fate. It was then, and then only, in this terrible trial, they displayed any nobility of spirit.

In compliance with these orders from Agra, a wing of the Sixtieth, a wing of the Carabineers, and a strong force of Artillery, marched for Delhi on the 25th of May, and Captain M. was left in command of the wing of his regiment that remained. As he, with the few officers present, was required to sleep where the men lay on their arms, I was left much alone.

The fatal results of war were soon brought to our door. In a few days the column was met on the Hindun by a Native force from Delhi, when the test regarded by many with so much anxiety was tried. Here, for the first time, British regiments met our Sepoy regiments as deadly enemies. The ground was chosen by the Natives, and their heavy artillery was most judiciously placed; but after a sharp action that artillery was captured, and the enemy was driven back into the city. On the following day a second division drew across the road to dispute the passage of the column; they also were driven in confusion over the river, and the King heard in his palace the roar of the guns, and saw the men, who boasted that on their arms rested the empire, broken like sheep by the master-hand that had taught them to conquer.

Doolies* of wounded men came back to the hospital, and amongst them a gallant young officer who had left us in high health and spirits, and whose life was now ebbing fast. Poor Napier was buried in the graveyard at Meerut, one of the earliest victims in battle of a war destined to swallow up a host. In that cemetery lie the victims of the first massacre, and near the bridge of the Hindun, to the right, as the traveller passes to Delhi, a mound covers the remains of those who first fell in the field. Under it rests Captain

* A light palanquin for carrying the sick.

Andrews, to whom I had just bid adieu. He was killed at the head of a party of his men, after the capture of the guns, by the explosion of an ammunition waggon; and one of the worst cases among the wounded was that of a soldier who was standing near him at the time. This man had been picked up more like a cinder than a human being, yet by care he recovered; and it was a pleasure for me to supply to him, and other brave men, many little delicacies permitted by the doctors.

The column passed up the Jumna, and crossed by a bridge of boats some twelve miles above the city, where they joined the Field Force. Not long after, this bridge was destroyed, and the left bank of the river fell into the possession of the rebels.

On the 8th June, the Field Force moved on Delhi; and at Budhe-ka-Serai, some three miles outside the walls, they found the enemy in position. After a well-contested action, the Sepoys were defeated for the third time, with the loss of their guns, and pursued to the walls of their stronghold. Then commenced a siege that will live long in history—a siege on which hung greater interests than on any other undertaken by our country, and the memory of which will last, a monument of the endurance and courage of the British soldier.

CHAPTER III.

Expected Attack on Meerut—Defensive Preparations—Warlike Rumours—My Khansumah and Ayah—Native Servants—Nunkin India—Beneficial Use of the Seventy-ninth Psalm—Massacre at Cawnpore—Effects of the Mutiny—Siege of Delhi—English Prestige—News of the Capture of Delhi reaches Meerut.

When the detachment from our garrison had crossed the river, the road became clear and open between the rapidly-increasing force of the mutineers and our cantonment. The spies of the "Intelligence Department" now constantly brought reports of the preparations at Delhi for the attack on Meerut. These accounts gave full particulars of the *durbars* held, the regiments ordered, the guns detailed, and the King's commands to the chief who was to direct the expedition. Spies were taken measuring the ditch, noting the guns, and our means of defence; and all held that it was more than probable that the attack would be made.

Immense preparations were commenced to repel the threatened assault; enormous fortifications arose around the Infantry barracks, enclosing the houses of the officers. Roads were cut across; the trees and mud walls of the compounds were cleared away from the front of the guns; masses of grain were stored; and a position was selected and strengthened on the open plain to meet the rebels on the march.

The extensive nature of these works imposed on the country, covered the real weakness of the position, and cowed the followers of the Mogul, who could find no general to command, or troops to undertake a service attended with so much danger.

A few lighted arrows fired into the thatched roofs of our barracks would have burnt us all out, and left us exposed to the deadly rays of the sun. But the mutineers had broken away from all discipline and control, and given themselves up to riot and plunder, and from the capital, thronged with well armed and trained soldiers, scarcely an enterprise demanding courage and vigour was undertaken. The entire district was left to us; expeditions were constantly going forth from Meerut, and the severe and summary punishment inflicted on the insurgent villages, kept in awe the unruly tribes of Goojurs around.

The tales of murder at Mooradabad, at Bareilly, at Agra, at Lucknow, of mutiny in the camp, of treachery even within our fortifications, kept us in a constant thrill of alarm. Now I heard of the overwhelming force of the rebels at Delhi, the death of the Commander-in-chief, the hopelessness of the siege, of the capture of Calcutta; then dim rumours of Cawnpore, of the rise of Oude and Rohilcund, of the murder of Sir John Lawrence, and the insurrection of the Punjab. Truth was strangely mixed with fable; some of the reports were wholly true, and most founded on probabilities. The real ignorance of events was harassing in the extreme, as our fate depended as much on circumstances occurring at extremities of the empire, of which we could gain no tidings, as on those that more nearly concerned us.

In all our hearts was a painful anxiety how the news from India would be viewed in England.

On that rested our ultimate preservation. If the nation, alive to the great emergency, put forth her mighty strength, we should be saved; if not, the chances were—we died. Month passed away after month, and the anxious desire for news from home grew in intensity. That Delhi should fall, that our country should rise in wrath and deliver India, were the daily prayers offered up by the British community, now fairly at bay throughout these provinces.

When the sun had set, the people assembled in the Dum-Dum in a circle, and the chaplain repeated prayers and portions of Scripture—his extraordinary memory enabling him to do this without the book. That concluded the day, and nothing was afterwards heard save the call of the sentries repeating from post to post the cry, "All's well."

My Khansumah, a bigoted Mussulman, became troublesome as the mutiny progressed. He entered with interest into the rumours current in the bazaars, and retailed them to his fellow-servants in the worst light.

When transacting his market business with me, he often inquired about the news from Agra, whither he seemed to turn most hopefully, and sometimes he ventured the remark that there was very bad news from that city. At the worst time of the siege of Delhi, he earnestly applied for a few days' leave, which I granted; and I was afterwards informed he employed the period in visiting the besieged town, and inspecting its means of defence, as well as the character of the operations directed against it. I noticed a change in his manner on his return, as if the piles of artillery, the pyramids of shot, and the racks of the great arsenal, filled up to the ceiling with small arms, had inspired him with confidence, and he could foresee the approach of Mussulman ascendancy, when Allah's name would resound over the land, and the followers of Mahomet alone be considered eligible for the loaves and fishes.

Among a people who find it difficult to tell a true tale, the stories circulated were more false than those in our circle. The wildest rumours gained ready credence with the Natives, and they firmly believed that our power in India was at an end. The Ayah, who looked upon the mutiny with dread, would come full of a tale of extermination she had obtained from the Khansumah, and I was obliged to warn him that his conduct might lead to serious consequences. The Ayah regarded the revolt from a professional point of view. "Who will give us bread?" she asked, "when the ladies and children are murdered or driven from the land?" She had heard that, before the English came, Natives of her class feared to wear good clothes, or to shew signs of comfort, for such display led to extortion by the followers of the Rajahs or Kawahs in whose districts they lived; and I am persuaded that the truth of this was felt by numbers of the lower classes.

From whatever cause, there can now be little question of the general fidelity of our servants during this trying period. Gentlemen speak in terms of high praise of the conduct of the Syces—always close to their master's horse even under fire—of the water-carriers, dooly-bearers, and others, besides the house-servants, many of whom fell in the campaigns. Our Mussulman water-carriers, however, left us during the gloomiest period to return to Mooradabad, then in the hands of the rebels, though much kindness had been shown to both, who were father and son.

It is certain that the assumption of power and confidence on the part of the English greatly swayed the Natives with whom they came in contact, and much contributed to the defeat of the revolt. The people were treated with extreme harshness, and the servants often met with bad usage. The good and evil qualities of our race told alike in our favour in the emergency. The courage and vigour—the haughtiness and stubborn pride—the insolence, and even the cruelty—half disdainful, half revengeful, all spread their influence around, and individual men thus upheld in whole districts the prestige of our rule. Not one act of revolt was committed by the people of Meerut after the 10th of May; and although numbers of them were executed, no signs of disaffection were shown.

Among those who had sought protection within our fortified circle were the nuns of the Convent of Sirdhana, a pretty place about ten miles from Meerut, the property of the late Dyce Sombre. Apartments in the hospital had been allotted to them, and I visited the Lady Superior. I was much struck with the beauty, and the calm, sweet manner of one of the sisters, Madame St. Anthony. She gave me an account of the mutiny at Sirdhana, of the tumultuous gathering of the

Natives, and the way they had threatened the convent. A man from the town offered them protection for one hundred and fifty rupees. While the Lady Superior was considering, another came forward with a similar demand. As such negociation was fruitless, they determined to trust alone in Providence. Calculating that plunder would be the chief object, they all assembled on the flat roof of the large building, and taking only the host with them, they awaited the result, when they were relieved by a party of volunteers from Meerut.

On my expressing sympathy for their alarm, she said, with a placid smile: "No alarm was felt, for they were prepared." However strongly her mind may have sustained her, she was physically unequal to such shocks, and I was deeply grieved, a few weeks after, to hear of her untimely death.

But these were days when death was, in many instances, a blessing. The very air of India was charged with horrors. The weary watching, the sickening expectation, and the wearing effects of the climate had a depressing tendency that required much resolution to struggle against, and all the consolations of religion to sustain. The men were relieved by action, but for the women there was not this resource. The Roman Catholic priests of Meerut directed the members of their church to repeat the seventy-ninth psalm with their daily devotions. When I heard this, I referred to David's beautiful song, and felt its thrilling and elevating influence, written as if in sole reference to our circumstances. Indeed, for sustaining power in trying positions, I believe the Psalms to be of mighty effect.

A regiment of Seikhs was detached to Meerut, and two hundred of the Rifles, one hundred Artillerymen, and the wounded who had recovered, were directed to join the camp before Delhi, and on the night of the 26th of August my husband left me, to command this party of his regiment.

I will not attempt to enlarge on my feelings during this most unhappy period of my life.

When the fortifications had been completed around the houses, we returned to our home, and after my husband had marched for Delhi, a young lady left the Dum-Dum to share with me its accommodation.

Though the inactivity of the Sepoys added to our confidence, and allowed of our emerging so far, still the country was considered most unsafe beyond our lines for any except armed parties.

The massacre of the garrison that surrendered at Cawnpore, of which we had garbled and unreliable accounts, had capped the folly and bloodthirstiness of the rebellion, had nerved every garrison with despair, and every field force with revenge, and had thus done more to defeat the object of the rebels than any other act of the sad drama. England owes more to the massacre at Cawnpore than perhaps she will readily believe. We knew that between us and this revolt there could be no terms, no quarter, no rest; and when we looked on the gigantic task before us, utterly to destroy the army we had made, it was no wonder that many despaired of the result. Myriads in India listened with the most eager anxiety for intelligence fron Delhi. Already tribes of Natives away on the borders of our empire were gathering their arms, and songs of exultation were beginning to arise from those who hated our rule.

Even close to our cantonment, a great brigade had passed, destroying the station of Hauffer, almost within sight, and marching in triumph to Delhi, with miles of hackeries containing the plunder of Rohilcund.

The sullen sound of the Delhi artillery seldom failed to reach a listening ear in Meerut. In the stillness of the night its low roar now came with a deeper meaning, and caused a greater emotion than before. The roar of an enemy's gun sounds strangely, and carries with it as great a thrill to the heart of the soldier who hears it for the first time, as to that of the citizen engaged in his peaceful pursuits.

But the siege was now hastening to its close. The great crisis had come; all the available force had been poured into the camp before the city, and it remained for General Wilson to take Delhi, or to lose India.

Those who know India can alone fully comprehend the situation. All through the crisis our sway was greatly upheld by the force of opinion. The effects of a long career of victory cannot be effaced in an hour. There is reason to believe the opposition would have been more general if both princes and people had not had an innate feeling of terror at exciting the wrath of the lordly lion, though half persuaded he was mortally wounded, and his days numbered. To maintain this feeling, an uninterrupted course of victory is necessary, or a blow so crushing, that the previous check only makes its effects more visible. Thus Aliwal and Sobraon were required to restore the drawn battles of Moodkee and Ferozeshah, which shook our power to its foundation. It is therefore incumbent on us to overcome all oppositions; for if a native ruler can erect a stronghold and successfully defy us, the country will quickly become covered with such fortifications, and our rule with contempt. A check in the field, a delay in the storm of a city, excites far and near the attention of hostile communities, and may raise a commotion that would require a combined effort of the nation to withstand.

During a period of such intense and wide-spread excitement, which fixed on the proceedings in India the wrapt attention of all its people, and of every nation of Asia, it became absolutely essential to re-establish our prestige by a stroke that smote into the dust the city most calculated to draw interest and to awake enthusiasm, and which had withstood our authority for many months. So the prestige that told against the revolt in one way, told against ourselves in another; for while it frightened many a prince into good behaviour, it made the capture of Delhi and the advance of Havelock necessities of our existence, though both extremities of war.

On the 7th of September the operations commenced that were to decide the momentous question, and on the 20th the British ensign floated over the imperial palace.

Short as was this interval, it was an age to me.

Although within sound of the guns, our intelligence was often inaccurate and unreliable. The mails carried round by Paneeput took days to reach us; but, on the morning following that great day,* when the columns advanced to the storm of Delhi, a native runner arrived with the news. He said he had been borne across the bridge of boats in a throng so great that his feet could scarcely touch the ground, and the country around was covered with the fugitive army and denizens of the imperial city.

As rumours to this effect had often been received, the man was secured, with the promise of reward if the account proved true; and if false, of a punishment which would have left him nothing more to hope for in this world. On receipt of

* The 14th September, 1857.

further news our joy was considerably modified. An entrance had, indeed, been effected, though with immense loss of life; and the force was still fighting for its existence in the streets of Delhi.

The deep, low sound which had spoken such volumes to my heart, had, indeed, ceased; yet I knew the warfare then going on to be more deadly, though less loud, and my anxiety was rather increased thun diminished.

The country was hushed—every ear was open—every head stretched forward for intelligence of this decisive struggle. Perhaps never before on so few British bayonets had hung so great a cause; and never before was news received in India by our race with more deep-felt joy, and thankfulness to our Heavenly Preserver, than that of the final and glorious close of this great siege.

Delhi was the lists where was fought out the challenge from the native army. The prize for the victor was India—for the vanquished, death.

When Delhi fell the failure of the mutiny was decided; and the after-campaign was a mere race of the vanquished from a pursuing fate.

It was not, however, the triumph to our arms, the display of British courage, nor the political results obtained, that so filled with thankfulness the English community in these provinces—our lives were wrapped up in the siege; the existence of every Christian depended on the success of our force; and though England might have re-conquered her Indian empire, had the attack failed, that empire, till such re-conquest, would undoubtedly have been lost.

CHAPTER IV.

Military Arrangements after the Fall of Delhi—Appearance of the City—The Palace—Fountains—The Peacock Throne—Scene of the Struggle—House of Sir Theophilus Metcalfe — The Cashmere Gate — The Chandnee Chowk—Effects of the War.

THE fall of Delhi opened a direct communication between Meerut and the Field Force; and several officers took the opportunity to pass to and from the captured city.

I need not tell the joy I felt to be awoke one night by my husband's arrival. It was decided that I should return with him; and on the evening of the 17th October we started, and reached Delhi on the following morning.

The battalion was quartered in the Palace, a word that will give a false idea to those who do not know the East.

The late residence of the Timour family is enclosed within a wall, three miles in extent, enormous in height, with bastions and fortified gates, embrasures and rows of loop-holes. It is faced with slabs of red sandstone, as if built of block, giving it a grand and massive appearance. Within this wall are the houses of the Emperor, mosques, halls of justice and of audience, garden with numerous summer-houses, and the court-yards pertaining to his Majesty. Yet these form only a part of the whole, as there are barracks for the three regiments the King was allowed to keep, and dwellings for retainers of all degrees, from the establishments of princes of the blood to the huts of the Coolies, making up a population of 10,000 persons. The rule of the Mogul had narrowed till this circle represented his dominions; but here he had reigned supreme, with the power, I believe, of life and death.

The principal gate, in grand proportions equalling any other in the world, faced the principal street of Delhi, called the Chandnee Chowk, or Silver Street.

When I entered, one of its massive portals hung a tottering ruin on a hinge, blown in by

Colonel Sir John Jones, when his column advanced to the capture, just four weeks before. The mouths of three great guns were pointed to the entrance, as when placed by the enemy for the reception of this column. A fine arcade, gaily painted, and lined on both sides with shops, leads to an open square. The doors of the stalls were riddled with bullets, and, instead of the *buinahs* * with their goods, they were filled with the flat, ugly faces of the little Goorkhas.

Two years before I had entered this arcade; then it was occupied by a crowd of the King's guard, and I was rudely forbidden to proceed without the written order of Captain Douglas, who lived over the gate where the family in this fearful rebellion had been savagely murdered.

In the centre of the square the road goes by a tank, and in this was perpetrated one of the massacres that it will take years to forgive. The women and children who escaped death on the 11th and 12th of May were, after many days' confinement, butchered there in cold blood; and this deed was sanctioned by the King in his own territory.

* Shopkeepers.

A paved road leads through an archway to a great gate on the right, facing another fine street, and on the left passes on to the Fort of Selimghur, lined by the dry bed of a canal which formerly supplied this fatal tank with water. The court was filled with captured guns, waggons, and army materials of all sorts, showing, by dents and broken wheels, marks of severe service. I saw the uniform of the Rifles on guard in a building we passed under, and then we entered a fine court, and faced a grand edifice called the Amm-Kass, or Hall of Justice, occupied by what the siege had left of the battalion. The way to the private courts of the King was through an arch on one side of the Amm-Kass, but we were driven to the other side, where I could see no exit. On the top of the Justice Hall I noticed a strange structure, but it appeared stranger still when I was told it was my new abode.

I was wondering how this position could be reached, when the gharry stopped, and I was led, by a passage broken through a house behind the Amm-Kass, to a flight of steps up to the top of a wall broad enough for a carriage drive. This singular road, elevated more than twenty feet, wound through the palace, to houses, and around courtyards. A few paces to the left, another range of large stone steps led under the quaint structure to a handsome court with a marble fountain in the centre, carved elaborately, and inlaid with cornelian, blood-stone, and agate. The golden letters of the inscription had been abstracted, some of the stones were picked out, and the fountain was dry, as were all in this palace, which had once sparkled so brilliantly with flowing and with jetting water.

But the house most interested me, and I confess to a chill of despair when I turned to examine it. What had formerly been for the King a pretty summer residence, was now for me a cold wintry ruin, without windows, without doors, without even a floor. A shell had torn up the pavement, and the huge rent in the walls, considering the perilous elevation, aroused an unpleasant feeling of insecurity. A closer inspection, and a little time for thought, enabled me to see how the place could be made habitable. Below, two rooms were large and lofty, and smaller ones branched from them; above, a quaint one-room construction stood on the roof, with its little courtyard facing the river, while that below looked towards the city. Thus house rose on house to a pinnacle, the architect having apparently played with bricks and mortar as children play with cards.

For some time I was busy superintending masons, painters, and carpenters, and renewing what seemed to be the decay of a century of neglect.

But the whole palace of the Moguls was a sad picture of dilapidation and dirt. Dirt overlaid everything, dimmed the brightness of paint, and sullied the purity of marble. Mud walls, erected without an apparent object, hid the choicest specimens of architectural beauty, and coats of whitewash covered blocks of sculptured stone. The first appearance raised a doubt if it were indeed the dwelling of Akbar, the residence of Shah-Jehan. A more correct knowledge of this celebrated seat of government showed that debased descendants filled the place of refined ancestors. On the Dewan-Kass are inscribed in gold the boastful lines which now form so singular a contrast to the fact, and are thus translated by Moore in "Lalla Rookh"—

> "If there be a Paradise on earth,
> It is this, it is this."

From my house, if it still stands, the view is grand in extent, in beauty, and in interest. The palace, the city, the country lay like a map at our feet; and in every direction we looked through a clear atmosphere on a panorama I believe to be unequalled in India.

The giant walls of the palace rose in a battlemented circle around; and from this high post in its centre we gazed on its gardens, its squares, its streets, and all its varied buildings. The grey old Fort of Selimghur frowned on the Jumna, which, coursing close to the city wall, there divided, and sent a rapid and romantic-looking stream between the dark turrets of the ancient fort and the gay red walls of the palace. The water was spanned by two bridges—one hoary as Selimghur, the other light and elegant as the palace—a singular contrast between grey age and gay youth.

Far as I could see, the Jumna came winding down through the rich and level country, running close by, and away into the distance, where its glancing waters borrowed the azure of the sky, and the muddy current became in hue as ultramarine.

The palace hung over the water; its battlemented wall ceased where it reached the scarped bank, which wound with the channel, rising from the water some twenty feet, and faced with blocks of stone. The ground within the palace was level with the top, and it was on the crest of this scarp that the Moslem architect had lavished all his skill; and the result, in its day, must have been one of rare and tasteful beauty.

Buildings were massed together, and piled on each other, with quaint projections and curiously carved windows jutting over the water; and among these, conspicuous in beauty, stood out the Dewan Kass.

A seat of solid crystal, like a block of massive ice, was placed in a window, which, from its delicate tracery, seemed spun from marble—a fit spot for such a seat, and not unworthy of him who styled himself "Ruler of the World."

Next to this, the waters of the river reflected the trees of a garden, and among them were domes and minarets, mosques and summer-houses, difficult to describe—all of them small, but of exquisite material and finish. It was from the island where stands Selimghur that this scene broke with so singular a beauty on the sight; from my elevation the plan was clear, but the details were lost.

What strikes a stranger most forcibly, is the way in which the Moslem artist had revelled in water. From a marble summer-house that looked along the crest of the scarp, a stream had flowed in a little cataract down an inlaid slab of this stone, still resting on its old incline, and, passing under the floor, had been conducted in a marble canal into a series of buildings adjoining the Dewan Kass, where it had filled marble fountains and had circled into marble baths. The canal was dry, and almost choked with rubbish, and the visitor now entered rooms whose singular construction amazed him, and could only be accounted for by the fact that they had been erected to receive the falling showers of fountains.

A large square tank stood in the centre of the garden, and from the middle rose a curious structure of red stone, connected with the bank by a bridge that now passed over its dry bed, on which a boat lay rotting. Straight paved walks, and straight lines of trees, gave a formal aspect to the grounds, quite out of character with the style of the houses. Still, from above, the deep foliage hid these defects. The whole presented a scene more of neglect, almost amounting to barbarism, than of ruin, and with the water was gone the life and glory of the place.

Beyond the decaying seat of these degenerate kings, I looked over a city more beautiful far, when thus seen, than any other I had yet beheld. Its small size, being enclosed within walls about seven miles in extent, placed it all before me. I could almost trace the line of fortifications, with its gates and bastions, in its entire circuit. The wide streets, the principal houses, not hidden in masses of green foliage, the mosques and the temples, marked distinctly the districts in which they were situated.

Straight before me the Chandnee Chowk, with its lines of trees, ran grandly up to the Lahore Gate, cutting the city into halves. To the left was a dense region of houses, where, from a slight elevation, conspicuous in its huge proportions, rose the Jumma Musjid, its dome towering over all roofs, and its two minarets raising their elegant spires far above the dome. In all directions from this great Moslem temple the streets branched away like a spider's web.

The region on the right had been evidently the fashionable quarter, and its great houses peeped here and there from behind the leaves of numberless trees. I looked into the arsenal, over the wall so gallantly defended on the 11th May, on the rows of cannon and piles of shot that remained, but the college beyond was concealed by the branching boughs. The church alone, of all the buildings, clearly shewed its dome, and held up above them its golden cross.

Far over the city the Flag-staff Tower, the Observatory, and Hindoo Rao's—names so familiar to all in India—standing on the brow of a rocky height, were sharply defined against the blue sky.

That height is now enshrined in history, and sacred to the British nation. Between it and this spot the great fight had been fought, every position had been contested, and every yard was over a grave. The whole way was strewn with the wreck left by the war—a wreck not visible from where I stood, for the scene, which had been beautifully laid out, looked as lovely now as it had done before that fatal May. The leaves were as green, the white road passed round the tower as if uninjured by a shell, and the ruin of Hindoo Rao's only added to the picturesqne effect.

I did not know, as I gazed, that scarcely a human being was left in the silent city at my feet.

All I yet knew of the war was confined to the losses of our own people by battle and exposure, and I was ignorant of the awful destruction that had overtaken the inhabitants. It had not occurred to me that there were sufferers greater than ourselves, with whom I ought to sympathize.

In the building beneath me, where the Mogul emperors had administered justice, were lodged the third, left after the perils of the siege, of that noble battalion which had marched on the 25th May from Meerut. The room, supported on a forest of pillars, was gigantic in size. The emperor ascended from a private staircase at the back, and entering a raised dais of beautiful marble exquisitely carved, seated himself on that great throne which became the prey of Nadir Shah, and whose noblest gem now sparkles among the jewels of our Queen.

This was the celebrated Peacock Throne, and that diamond the Koh-i-noor.

Here it was the emperors held their public durbars, met ambassadors and administered justice; but the private audience was in the Dewan Kass, rising, as I have said, from the scarped bank of the river, and looking down on the Jumna. In that hall the last emperor was tried by a commission of British officers, where, not many years before, he had considered himself disgraced, and a stain cast on his escutcheon, because a Governor-General, and one of England's highest nobles, had sat down in his presence.

Shortly after my arrival, I drove over the field of the recent struggles. The advanced batteries had not yet been removed, though Coolies were beginning the work. The country was pretty between the walls and the hills, circling together for more than a mile, and maintaining an average breadth of about the same distance, the space between being tastefully laid out and intersected by roads which here and there were rough with the boulders that had rolled from the rocky height, and overgrown with a tangled vegetation. The air was fresh and exhilarating, and all looked bright on this autumn morning. The road passed close by the round Flag-Staff Tower, which I had looked on with interest from my elevated residence. The women and children assembled there, when the mutineers arrived from Meerut and the Delhi brigade, joined them in open rebellion.

Behind the circling hill was the ruined cantonment, and the long lines could still be traced where the tents of the British force had stood. A good road runs along the crest of the hill, and, passing the Observatory, we drove by it to a ruin of great interest. This was the solid and handsome house of Hindoo Rao, a wealthy native gentleman, who had given his name to the principal post of the besieging army, and the scene of innumerable combats. The entire front had been battered to pieces, and it was owing to the solidity of the structure that any portion of it still stood. The rooms so long occupied by the gallant little Goorkhas were pointed out to me, and a small apartment behind, where a shot from Kissen-gungje had burst, killing or dreadfully wounding nearly every one in the room. But Hindoo Rao's had been the scene of so many tragedies, the death-place of so many brave soldiers, that this shot is only remarkable for the wholesale nature of the destruction it effected. The ground was torn up by the projectiles and shot, and pieces of shell lay thickly strewn around.

Looking down on the city, the eye rested on the Moree Bastion, the destroyer of Hindoo Rao's, now itself a heap of ruins; and half-way between, as it appeared to me, a swarm of Coolies were at work demolishing the battery that had smashed the bastion into an undistinguishable mass.

The long line of wall between the Lahore and the Cashmere gates seemed little injured, but at the wall neared the Cashmere Gate, the effects of the fire were more apparent.

The singular beauty of Delhi was seen to even greater advantage from Hindoo Rao's than from the structure at the top of the Amm Kass. It combined the grace of Moslem architecture with the charm of English finish. Through trees and bungalows wound smooth Macadamized roads; beyond were the fortifications; still further away rose domes and minarets; and behind all were the dark red walls of the palace. From green trees peeped the roofs of houses, and these were broken by spires and pagodas; and I feel sure that, even during the worst period of peril and of anxiety, many who looked from that height, with the fierce determination utterly to destroy the city, must have acknowledged in their hearts that its beauty was beyond that of any other they had seen.

The hill from Hindoo Rao's slopes down to the Subsi-Mundi, and I passed on the way two or three batteries, such as the "Crow's Nest," with whose name I was familiar. At the base of the hill ran the high road between Delhi and Umballa, and beyond was the suburb of Kissengungje held by the enemy during the siege, and where the 4th column of assault had been repulsed with so terrible a loss.

The Subsi-Mundi is a large square Serai, and was the point on the extreme right of the British position. The operations of the force were conducted between it and the river Jumna; but the enemy had a battery on the right enfilading the height, and a battery on the left throwing its shot across the river. Thus, the besiegers were themselves besieged, and the beleaguered city had by far a wider scope of communication thån the beleaguering force.

On our return, we passed the handsome house of Sir Theophilus Metcalfe, now a sad picture of wanton destruction. Between it and the Cashmere Gate, this cruel war had everywhere left its mark; cannon-balls had splintered walls, and cut trees to pieces; shells had dug holes in the road, and every log of timber was penetrated by a stray bullet. The houses were in ruins, but the ruin in the country was mere play when contrasted with that in the town.

The fortifications were shattered, the gates lay on the ground, the bridge across the moat bore heavy traces of the strife, and the neighbourhood showed how large a portion of the fire had been concentrated on the Cashmere Gate.

This gate was the scene of some striking incidents of the mutiny. By it the troops advanced from the cantonment to meet the mutineers from Meerut. There the officers first became convinced how little the Sepoys they led were to be relied on; many escaped over the adjacent walls, and above it a British magistrate is said to have been hanged. There gallantly had died most of the party who had blown in the gate, and up that incline had rushed the assaulting column.

Where I stood had first rung the cheers of the British army on the day when the fate of India was placed in their hands. It is singular to relate that on this spot, not long after, a starving multitude of Natives—when the country groaned under a famine—were fed by British hands, from the proceeds of British charity; a noble sequel to the sad story, and one, I trust, that may be remembered to England's honour, if the acts of her sons during this dreadful period were not always tempered with justice and with mercy.

The first building of importance within the gate —the Protestant church—had not escaped a tremendous battering, though the chaplain declared that the cross that surmounted the dome was uninjured. The Delhi Gazette press, the college for native students, the houses of Khan Mahommed Khan, and of Colonel Skinner, were either totally destroyed or much damaged, and the walls and the ground were pitted with the marks of bullets and of shells.

Farther on, we passed the magazine Lieutenant Willoughby so gallantly attempted to destroy. Up a street to the right, bearing marks of the severe struggle, we entered a garden, with the remains of a splendid house standing in the centre. When the mutiny began it was occupied by the Delhi Bank, and became the tomb of the manager and of all his family. The murderers had rioted there in plunder and in destruction, and on it Brigadier Campbell had fallen back, after his brilliant advance to the walls of the Jumma Musjid. It had been strongly fortified, and was still covered by sand-bags, as it had been held during the period of the street-fighting, from the 14th September to the occupation of the palace.

A short street led into the Chandnee Chowk, a more melancholy picture still than any I had yet seen. When last I looked on this fine street, not many months before, it presented a gay and joyous sight; broad as it is, it was scarcely broad enough for the throng that filled it. Elephants and camels, horses and carriages, decked with the finery of the East, crowded the way; now, it was silent and empty. The contents of the shops lay strewn in the street, or huddled in a confused mass on the floors. The sneaking figure of some prowling thief, a lean, half-famished dog, or one of the many cats—the sole inhabitants of Delhi—were all that moved. The painful effect of this solitude was more depressing than even the ruin. Where were the people of Delhi? The tender children, the delicate women, the old and infirm—all were gone—swept away by the fatal crimes of others!

Those who know war, not from books, but from the experience of its realities, shrink from it with horror; and a war like this, without quarter and without mercy, is the worst affliction that can overtake a land. No city desolated by a plague ever wore the appearance of Delhi at that time, or became the solitude that it then was.

Before many months elapsed nearly every great city in the immense central provinces of India was stormed or occupied by our army; and the loss of life, the destruction of property, the cruel sufferings, will never be known to the world unless a second Macaulay wholly devotes himself to the task.

Right in the centre of the Chandnee Chowk a hideous erection of wood was the only new and uninjured structure—and this was the gallows. Hundreds perished on that platform, and among the number were rajahs and nawabs who had themselves, and their fathers before them, ruled in the territory around. I trust no innocent men died there, victims to the fierce hatred which the massacre had excited.

A war like this, however, acts with the fellest injustice; and were the number of blameless persons who were sacrificed, truly estimated, the British public would be horrified at the result. When Captain M. was visiting the advanced posts on the capture of Bareilly, he was asked by the officer in command what was to be done with some women who had been taken out of a well. The officer led him into a small enclosure, where, stretched on the ground, lay the dead bodies of six or seven girls, who evidently belonged to the upper classes. Beside them were five or six others slowly recovering, and an old woman rocking herself on her knees and pouring out her sorrows in prayer. The officer pointed to a narrow well, and down the black depths of this Captain M. looked, but could see no bottom. They had precipitated themselves into this hole, springing down one after another, amid the crash of shell and storm of shot preceding the advance of the troops to the capture of the city.

CHAPTER V.

Our Residence in the Captured City—Provisions—The English Mail—Want of Enterprise of the Gwalior Contingent—Search for Treasure—Concealment—Thirteen Waggons laden with Spoil—Jewelry and Precious Stones Captured—Miniatures—The Great Mogul a Prisoner—His Family—Commission for the Trial of Native Prisoners of Rank—Their Fate—Major Hodson—Conduct of the Royal Captives—The Jumma Musjid.

When the workmen had finished, we were in possession of a good sitting-room, dining-room, and bed-room, with a dressing-room at either end. The building was too much exposed for comfort in the season now approaching. It was not till the end of November that I really knew what the cold of a Delhi winter morning was. The wind howled through every crevice, and whirled the dust in eddies around the outer court. At night it whistled loudly around the corners of my singular house, and piles of blankets failed to keep me warm. In the day I heaped up logs on the low-lying fire, and this threw out a strong heat. The climate, during the winter, is fine, dry, clear, cold, and invigorating. People, unacquainted with India, picture to themselves the country for the whole year under a tropical sun, but they have little idea either of the fierceness of the heat in summer, or of the chilness of the blasts of winter, in the north-west provinces.

The supplies were abundant, and we experienced no difficulty, from the commencement of the war, in procuring all we required. English stores of course rose enormously; but everything grown in the country remained cheap and plentiful. A fowl could be purchased for a shilling, a dozen eggs one shilling and threepence, mutton and beef about sixpence per pound. Vegetables and fish were cheaper still; while hares, snipe, and wild-fowl were abundant in the market. The Chandnee Chowk began to re-assume some appearance of life, and while the rest of Delhi was a wilderness, shops and stalls were open there to supply the force quartered in the city.

No English mail had yet reached us, though news came by indirect sources, and we were gratified to learn how deep was the interest excited throughout the civilized world by the ardent struggle of the English in India. England had hastened to our rescue—the sea was covered with steamers full of troops. Batteries of Artillery and squadrons of Cavalry were pouring in by the overland route, and Sir Colin Campbell had assumed the command-in-chief. From other parts came intelligence of the advance of Havelock, the relief of Lucknow, and the victories of Sir Hugh Rose; and we looked hopefully for the time when this devastating war would cease.

The ignorance and folly of the men who had originated the mutiny became more strikingly displayed as it progressed to its close. The Gwalior Contingent, which had hung like a threatening cloud over the Delhi Field Force, and which for such a period could have decided by a move the fate of the siege, and consequently of India, marched, when Delhi had fallen, and Lucknow had been relieved, and we heard of the fierce battle they had fought at Cawnpore, and afterwards of their total defeat by the Commander-in-chief. It was by such acts of folly on the part of our enemy that we were saved in the great crisis. This war was begun by the Sepoys in treachery, ingratitude, and cruelty; was continued in ignorance and incapacity, without energy and without courage; and ended, not bringing to the surface one redeeming trait, or one man fit to rule.

The work carried on with most interest was the search for prize. Agents had been elected before the capture, and were diligently employed in gathering the booty, but the greater portion was lost through ignorance of its whereabouts.

They commenced by seizing the horses, carriages, and furniture—things that could not be concealed. The troops had entered the city calculating the booty at millions of rupees, but where these rupees were, none save the Natives had an idea. The knowledge dawned on us when the greater part had been abstracted by those better informed. The budmashes knew the rich houses, and where the coin was likely to be concealed, and they worked diligently in the dead of night. The prize agents employed a number of officers in the search. For a short period it became a most exciting pursuit, and my husband was actively and successfully engaged. After an early breakfast, he would start, with a troop of Coolies, armed with picks, crowbars, and measuring-lines. A house said to contain treasure would be allotted for the day's proceedings, and the business would commence by a careful survey of the premises. The houses enclosed a large extent of ground, generally containing two or three courts. The rooms faced on the courts, which were usually planted with grass, and shaded with shrubs. The houses seldom rose above one storey, with flat roofs, and staircases leading up to them, greatly facilitating the survey. By a careful measurement of the roofs above, and of the rooms below, any concealed space could be detected. Then the walls were broken through, and if there was a secret room, or a built-up niche, or recess, it would be discovered, and some large prizes rewarded their search.

On one occasion I had asked a few friends to lunch, expecting Captain M. home, when a guest informed me that there was no chance of his return, as a large treasure he could not leave had been found. It was late when he came back, with thirteen waggons, loaded with spoil, and, among other valuables, 80,000 rupees; in English money,

£8,000. On another occasion, after thoroughly ransacking a house, and obtaining silver vessels and gold ornaments, before the party withdrew a Cooly was directed to drive his pick into the grass of the court, and the first stroke went through a bag of a thousand rupees. Planted side by side in a neat border, under the earth, these bags were laid around the enclosure, but the canvas was so rotten, and the night so dark, that the work could not be finished, and it was impossible, without sleeping over the treasure, to preserve it to the agency. Hours would be lost in detecting and digging from the chunammed floors ponderous iron boxes, to find them empty; but the keenest disappointment was in the way the city was plundered by those not working for the army. Days were spent in ascertaining where a treasure had been hid, only to learn that the prize was gone, most probably to some of the ruffians who had aided in the plunder of the cantonment, and who had imbrued their hands in the blood of the victims of Delhi.

The tent where the more valuable articles were displayed, was pitched on the flat roof of a house overlooking the court of the Dewan Kass. There were several iron strong boxes among a miscellaneous collection, bearing trace of having been buried; and on chairs, sofas, and tables were shawls, silks, kincobs, swords, daggers, fans, and fowling-pieces. A prize agent opened one of the iron chests, and I saw pearls, emeralds, rings, and jewelry of every kind. Glass was mixed with precious stones of great worth, and pearls that required a practised eye to detect that they were false.

Often there was something paltry in the richest ornament. In a crown of pure gold, found by my husband in the palace of the empress, there were drops of green glass to represent emeralds. Silver vessels were sold for their weight in rupees, and at this rate an officer of the Carabiniers purchased a massive tea-pot of spurious metal, under the impression that it was silver. The native jewelry was pure in metal, but uncouth in form; diamonds and emeralds, large but flat; and although they excel in Delhi in filigree work, and can copy English patterns, yet the setting of these jewels was generally very coarse.

I was much interested in a collection of miniatures and portraits of Europeans, found during the search. Many of them had belonged to the murdered, and the agents wished them to be recognised and restored to those who prized them. There were bibles and prayer-books, with the names of ladies who had perished in the fly-leaf. And neither the palace of the King, nor the house of the Queen, was exempt from these relics, which so strongly condemned them.

The Great Mogul was now our prisoner, and lodged in a small house within the palace. Shortly after Delhi fell, the Royal family had been captured, and brought in by Major Hodson. He had shot on the spot two of the King's sons and a grandson. The eldest of these princes was a fine young man—the grandson a mere stripling; but if half the stories told of this boy be true, he was one of the most depraved monsters nursed by the mutiny.

Enough was elicited on the King's trial to show how dissipated and reckless these young men had been. Instead of leading in the field the revolted regiments that had proclaimed their father emperor, they headed the mutiny only in its murders and in its outrages. The petitions of the people for protection, and the records of the siege kept by the Natives, prove that though they shrunk from no unlawful act, they recoiled with fear and trembling from meeting our army in battle. The bodies of these ill-fated princes were carried to Delhi, and exposed in the Chandnee Chowk.

It was remarkable how fatal this mutiny was to all who took a leading part in it—to us as well as to the enemy. Nearly every Native prince or noble who led in the war against us either fell in battle, or perished by the hand of the executioner; and the number of our own leaders who were killed in the field, or sank under the fatigues of the campaign, has been a subject of deep grief to the nation.

A commission was sitting for the trial of Native prisoners of rank, and the Nawab of Jhugghur and the Rajah of Bolubghur had already perished by its sentence. The estates of these gentlemen lay on the Agra side of Delhi, in a district wholly in the hands of the rebels. The choice between the English, who might again come into power, and the mutineers, who were in power, was one of great difficulty to Natives acting without fixed principles, and inclining to that side they expected to be most to their advantage. For months the scales had been equally balanced; the prestige of empire was with us, but the belief throughout the land was that our sway had ended. With them the essence of politics is to temporise, and they had no true conception of the real character of their rulers.

From their infancy they had been accustomed to the mild Government of England, and they looked, at the worst, for interminable law proceedings. Acting on this conviction, at the same time that they furnished the King of Delhi with the sinews of war, they endeavoured to keep up a communication with the English General. Unfortunately for them, when the King deserted his palace he left evidence strewed about sufficient to convict them—papers that told a strange tale. That such proof against his supporters, which he had ample time to destroy, should have been left open and exposed, was a remarkable act. Similar instances occurred during the war, and furnish another of the unaccountable proceedings of this unaccountable people.

The Nawab was in Delhi when the mutineers entered from Meerut, and he was much blamed for not aiding our people with his numerous followers. He replied to this, with startling justice, "that it was England who had armed and trained the ruffians that had brought the calamity on the land; and it was not fair to expect him to compel that obedience in his followers which the rulers of the country and his judges had failed in compelling among their own."

This prince met his fate on the gallows with a calmness, a fortitude, and gentlemanly bearing that inspired my husband, who commanded the escort, with the deepest respect.

More melancholy still was the death of the Rajah, whose sympathies as a Hindoo were probably as much with the English as with the Moslem Emperor. Gentle in manner, young and handsome in person, it was the hard fate of this noble to be placed in circumstances wherein every path was fraught with peril, and to be tried when death was the award of any act hostile to our rule. There was something touching in the last words he spoke before his judges—"I was securely seated on a goodly bough of a flourishing tree, and my own act has sawn asunder the branch on which I rested."

The King's turn had come to appear before this fatal tribunal, and all were anxious to see how the old man would deport himself on the trying occasion. The Commission sat in the Dewan Kass —that private hall of reception sacred to him, and which the etiquette of the Court for centuries had forbidden any to enter, except by command. Not often even in history has such an instance of the vanity of human power been seen, as when this representative of one of the greatest houses was arraigned for high crimes before a few British officers—not one of whom held the substantive commission of Lieutenant-Colonel.

As he was borne through the arch of the inner court, the unhappy sovereign might have observed two cleverly executed outlines in chalk on the wall of the recess, which, in the days of his prosperity, the guard nearest his person had occupied. Both were so strikingly like his sharp aquiline face and attenuated form, that the words written beneath were unnecessary to convey to any one who had seen him the meaning of the drawings. "The King of Delhi as he is," was under the first; the other represented him hanging from a gibbet, and beneath it was written—"The King of Delhi as he ought to be."

The proceedings were opened by an able and eloquent address from the Judge-Advocate-

General, in which he spoke to the charges against the King. The trial was one of investigation, and the court would come to a finding, but had no power to pass sentence. They would record evidence, now the opportunity offered, that would eventually be of great historical interest, besides finally determining how far the King was really culpable.

Then the fallen monarch appeared under an escort of riflemen, and his palanquin was carried into the hall. He was accompanied by Jumma Buckt, the child of his old age, and of his wife Zenud Mull, now almost the only survivor that remained to him of his family. Before him sat the Commission by whose stern sentence so many of that family had already perished, and the guards around him wore the uniform of the soldiers beneath whose bullets they had fallen. The feeble old man rested on a pile of cushions. He was short in stature, and of a slight and infirm figure; his face was handsomely cut, the nose prominent and aquiline, the features intelligent, and with an air of refinement that did not disgrace his high descent. The trial had been postponed from week to week by his illness, and was now delayed by frequent adjournments to give him time for repose. At first he appeared alarmed, and his face wore an anxious expression; but by degrees it became more vacant, and he assumed or felt indifference, remaining apparently in a state of lethargy, with his eyes closed, during the greater part of the proceedings.

One of the chief questions was, whether the King had sanctioned the murder of the Christians who had escaped the first massacres; and I believe the Commission found that his order for the execution had been obtained. It appeared from what I gathered that he had condemned the conduct of the Nana at Cawnpore; and there was abundant proof that he had striven hard to protect the citizens of Delhi from the violence of the soldiery and the outrages of the nobles, and the people in the country from the plundering Goojurs.

It was clear how wretched the old man had been when eddied about in the whirlwind of the mutiny, with no energy to control, and no force of will to rule the cruel natures around. Numerous petitions from the people were translated, with the King's remarks. Much of what he said was sound and good, but his complaints were bitter of the insolence of the Sepoys, who had so cringed to us.

How keenly he felt the thorns in the bed which had been prepared for him! He was a mere puppet, who had drifted down a stream, and suddenly found itself the most prominent object in a great sea of trouble.

I cannot think that in the treatment of the last of the house of Timour our country showed her usual liberality. We must keep the fact ever before us, that it was *our* army that set the country in a blaze—that it was our timidity that led to the great catastrophe; and we have not even the excuse that the mutiny was an unforeseen event.

Some weeks before the outbreak, my husband repeated a conversation he had held with Mr. Hodson, afterwards the celebrated leader of "Hodson's Horse," who said: "Some years ago I was at a public dinner given to a Governor-General of India. In drinking his health an allusion was made to the campaign on the Sutledge, and in reply he observed: 'Trust me, gentlemen, that your greatest war is to come, and that war will be with your own Native army.'" Mr. Hodson added, "I was even then impressed with the truth of this remark, and I now believe that the predicted war is drawing near."

A few months only elapsed when that good soldier himself fell in the contest he had foreseen.

Amid all the poverty and contempt thrown on the King, I was gratified to observe the demeanour of many of the witnesses when called to give evidence. Bowing to the ground, with hands clasped, before the miserable figure on the bed, addressed by them as "Ruler of the Universe," though by the Commission as *tum*,* they observed to the powerless old man a degree of respect they denied to the court who had only to nod the signal for their execution.

Many of the ladies who arrived in Delhi paid a visit of curiosity to the Queen, but I was deterred by the report that her Majesty regarded these as visits of respect. I had no respect for the character of Zenud Mull. I therefore refrained from gratifying my curiosity. The demeanour of her son, young Jumma Buckt, on the trial of his father, was an exhibition of bad taste, and in striking contrast to that of the old servant who attended the King.

The residence of the Empress in the days of her

* Pronounced *toom*—thou; a mode of address only used to inferiors and servants.

prosperity was situated in the city, at some distance from the palace. The house is a fair sample of the dwellings of the grandees in Delhi, and one day I accompanied my husband to inspect the mansion. Part of the building stood on the street, three stories high. I passed under an archway by outhouses into a passage leading into an oblong court, with buildings facing me around. A canal ran through the centre of the court, with the usual fountains, and the ground was laid out as a garden.

The buildings were one-storeyed, with a flat roof; a row of rooms opened to the court, and another row was behind them. The apartments of the Queen were at the ends of the parallelogram, tastefully decorated. A large portion of the prize had been taken in this house, and in the search the agents had turned it upside down. Broken china strewed the floors, torn drapery and articles of little value covered the court, piles of earth shewed where holes had been dug, and walls, with great openings dashed through them, proved that no difficulties had stood in the way. By a side door I went into a smaller court, and from that into another, none of them alike. Then I came to a range of outhouses and of stabling. The extent was considerable, though the accommodation was not great.

The Jumma Musjid holds the same rank in India that St. Peter's does in the Roman Catholic world. Like St. Paul's, it stands in the heart of the city, on slightly rising ground. The plateau from which the walls arise is a stupendous structure, and the steps and gateway are worthy of the plateau. When there, the visitor is in a vast open court, paved with blocks of sandstone—the material of the building, excepting the domes and minarets, which are composed of marble. From one of the tall spires he looks over the country as from a balloon, and like a novice at the mast-head he wonders how the slight column can bear him aloft. The old ruins around Delhi, away to the Kootub, eleven miles off, are visible from this spot.

Delhi was a great city before the Moslem set foot in Hindostan, and for ages it has swayed backwards and forwards on the banks of the Jumna, within range of this view. Upon a rocky soil, plentifully supplied with stone, many traces must remain of so ancient a city; and ruins are everywhere to be found, of which the most remarkable is the Kootub. This exquisite tower, like the Taj, is the most perfect work of its kind; but the tower is so old, and its history so obscure, that it loses much of the interest attaching to the mausoleum. The summit of that tower, from which I also gazed, has its own tragic story of the mutiny; for some of the retreating Sepoys, who there sought refuge, were hurled from the top.

With the first of the year, officers began to arrive from England, and again the communication was opened along the great military road. As yet, however, it was only the Doab that was cleared of the mutineers, for all the country on the left bank of the Ganges was in arms, and there was little but rebellion on the right bank of the Jumna.

The battalion received its orders to march to Meerut on the 1st of February. The bundles of our servants had greatly increased, and their demand for carriage was now on a most extravagant scale. The bearer who had been of service during the mutiny had lately been found impossible to move; he had taken up his residence in a room at the foot of our entrance steps, and he feared to leave the spot, where he kept watch over his plunder. The cares of riches were now embarrassing him, and the robber dreaded being robbed. Having a wholesome fear of the Prize Agents, he did not appear in kincobs and satins until after his return to Meerut; but then he turned out in princely costume; grandeur such as his could not be expected to work. So he passed away like a comet, and I bethought me of the old saying, "It is an ill wind that blows nobody good."

CHAPTER VI.

Return to Meerut—Convalescent Depôts—Entrance into Rohilcund of the Roorkee Field Force—The Base of the Himalayas enclosed by the Ganges—General Jones's Force—Crossing the Ford—Mistakes of the Sepoys—They are attacked by the Advancing Column in the Centre of the Terai—Flight of the Nawab—Attack on the Enemy's Position before Mooradabad, and their Defeat—Khan Bahadour Khan—Relief of Shahjehanpore—Sir Colin Campbell—Tremendous Heat.

THE road from the palace was lined with the gallant little Goorkhas as the Rifles passed out on their return to Meerut, and the chilly air rang with the cheers of their old companions in arms.

At this time rest was unknown in India, the country being in commotion with moving columns —and the war, hitherto local, was now general throughout the land. It is seldom that so wide a field of operations has been seen; and it was necessary to make up by constant movement for the want of numbers, though a stream of troops had been poured into Hindostan by both the sea and the overland routes.

We had scarcely settled in our old house before a wing of the 60th joined a force under General Penny on the march to Kassgungje, and my husband left Meerut in command of the Rifles, and once more I was alone. But life now in the cantonment was greatly changed from the days when he had gone to the siege of Delhi. Scarcely a trace remained of the fortifications, and though gloom still hung over the bazaars, the roads were again gay with carriages, and the station had returned to its pristine ways.

It is difficult for those who live at home at ease, fully to realise the relief a feeling of security brings. Every-day blessings are the greatest, though the least appreciated, until they are lost, and there are many whose full value can never be known in Great Britain; for our country is so happily constituted that I believe they cannot be lost. During the weary months I had last passed at Meerut, how ardently I had hoped to enjoy an existence free from this weight of danger, this depressing, never-ceasing anticipation of a dreadful fate—felt during the day and during the night, asleep and awake; a sword suspended over the head, embittering every enjoyment of life. Often my imagination carried me far from this distracted land, and pictured the happiness of an English fireside—of home and safety.

Although this absolute security was denied, still I contrasted with thankfulness the comparative freedom from danger both of the English in these provinces, and of the service in which the troops were engaged. Before, under a scorching sun, the men, isolated far in Asia among hosts of enemies, had gone forth to a task of desperation; now, the rebellion had been met, checked, rolled back, and the voice of encouragement, of sympathy, and of assistance came with an earnest sound from our country, and met an eager welcome.

In the interval of my husband's absence, the joyous news reached me that he was named for the command of one of the Convalescent Depôts on the Himalayah mountains; but the appointment was not to be taken up until the service required from the battalion had been completed. It soon appeared that the Commander-in-chief had views for the 60th, incompatible with the detachment of the wing under General Penny. That wing was directed to march on Roorkee, the great engineer station, where a strong force had been for some time assembling. Then the Commander-in-chief's plan was made known to the Colonel, who was ordered to march the remainder of the battalion to Roorkee, and assume command of the column, now designated "The Roorkee Field Force." At the same time, he was gazetted a Brigadier-General, and desired to select a staff, and he named my husband his D. A. Adjutant-General.

The proceedings of this force will afford my readers more interest than a detail of the stupid life I myself led at Meerut, and I therefore give a general idea of the campaign that followed, gained from letters, telegrams, and despatches.

The Roorkee Field Force crossed the Ganges, and entered Rohilcund below the pilgrim city of Hurdwan, where the clear stream debouches from the hills, and hurries over a stony bed into the alluvial soil of the plains.

Along the foot of the Himalayah runs a belt of forest land inundated in the rainy season, and always covered with a tropical vegetation—a region of fever and a den of wild beasts. In droves the towering elephant crushes down the underwood—the crouching tiger hides in the thickest lairs—and the screech of the hyena, and the howls of wolves and of jackals, are heard without cessation through the night. In so fit a region were enacted some of the tragedies of these bad times. The advancing footsteps of the British army pressed back the native troops into this wilderness, and the Nana, with many of the leaders, and a crowd of followers, is said to have perished there from the deadly effects of the climate.

From Hurdwan the Ganges takes a wide bend, enclosing between its waters and the ranges of the Himalayah the country forming the provinces of Rohilcund and of Oude. This tract is, perhaps, the fairest in India. The great mountains that rear their icy crests along its length, roll many streams through its plains to the sacred river—plains level as a bowling-green, and fertile as those of Lombardy. With the exception of the belt I have described, it is well cultivated, well wooded, and covered with goodly cities.

Such were the newly-acquired kingdom of Oude

and our old province of Rohilcund, where the mutiny erected its strongholds, and whence it drew its chief strength.

When the Doab had been cleared, and the right bank of the Ganges was in our hands, Sir Colin placed a cordon from the hills at Hurdwan to the territory of Nepaul, and having fixed his nets, he drew in his prey. The rebels had the option of retiring into the belt I have described, called the Terai, or of breaking through his lines; but neither course held out much hope of escape. It was, in reality, death from disease, or death by the sword, that was offered.

The columns were put simultaneously into motion, and although acting many hundreds of miles apart, the movements were so directed that they converged together on the city of Bareilly about the central spot.

General Jones's force was, therefore, not an independent column, but a portion of an army acting on the enemy's flank, and one skilfully placed by his Excellency, and ably directed by its commander. It was required to sweep the land from the point where the river cuts through the Terai, while General Penny held a post in the centre, and Sir Colin, in command of a splendid force, advanced from the south-east. The fords of the Ganges were well guarded. As the Roorkee Field Force came down from the north-west, his Excellency drew up from the south-east, and, as they closed, General Penny crossed the river and pushed on for the capital.

The enemy, distracted by the advancing dangers, offered no combined resistance. Khan Bahadoor Khan, who reigned at Bareilly, only attempted to stop Sir Colin's advance when his guns were within reach of the city, and he was there totally defeated. General Penny was killed on his march from the river to join the Commander-in-chief.

But the most successful of these columns was that under Brigadier-General John Jones, who proudly boasted no gun was pointed at him that he did not capture, and who inflicted so signal a punishment on the mutineers, that he received in India the *sobriquet* of the Avenger.

When the Roorkee Field Force crossed the Ganges it entered the Terai; and here the enemy committed one of those many mistakes made by the Sepoys, which prove that, however defective may have been our own intelligence, theirs was still worse.

It was some time before the material could be collected for throwing a bridge across the river, and a small party was detached from Roorkee to guard the men engaged in the work. The enemy moved a force through the forest from a ford they held in strength opposite the city of Nujeebabad, probably to demolish both the party and the work. In the centre of the Terai they came in contact with the column, in full march to attack their position, and the shock was fatal to the rebels. They lost all their material, and left hundreds in the thickets to be devoured by wild beasts. The prestige of the rebellion, also, in these parts was destroyed. The Natives, who would not believe a simple truth—who were ignorant of passing events to an inconceivable extent, and credited an enemy's success only when he was at their door—saw the men who had so long boasted of their prowess emerge from the forest in a panic, without arms, and many even without clothes.

No attempt was made to defend Nujeebabad. The Nawab fled from his palace, which was destroyed, and his strong fort surrendered without a blow.

Before the troops had passed through the deserted city, the camp followers, like a swarm of noxious insects, darted on their prey. In a short time the town and the surrounding country were in flames, and the General beheld with dismay the first results of his operations in the destruction of the fair country he had entered. He seemed to have let loose on the unhappy land a legion of fiends; but he had the power to bind as well as to loose, and the energetic measures adopted saved the province.

English people can scarcely believe in the wickedness of actual war. Its civilized and legitimate operations are terrible enough, but without an iron hand to repress, there is no cruelty, no crime, however dreadful, that will not be enacted under its shade. The first day's operations left a crowd of wounded to an awful death; the next two or three saw a city deserted and destroyed, the villages around in a blaze, and the country covered with men as ready to murder as to steal, and bent on destruction. If the extermination of the province were aimed at, the General had but to protect the plunderers, and without the aid of a soldier the land throughout its length and breadth would have become a howling wilderness. Some of the dreadful men who perpetrated these enormities stole away from the ranks of the army, numbers came from among its followers, but the country itself furnished the most—and sad as this truth is, I fear it would be true of all countries.

Between Nujeebabad and Mooradabad is a town called Nugeena, with a canal flowing in its front. The enemy fell back on it, and from the fords of the Ganges and the country around their troops assembled, and drew up between Nugeena and the canal, to dispute the passage of the Field Force. The General heard with pleasure that his enemies were gathering together, and waited a few days, both to give them time and to allow his siege-train to be carried across the ford from Roorkee.

At midnight, on the 21st April, the British troops got under arms, and about eight o'clock the advanced guard passed over the bridge of the canal. The head of the column halted on the bridge, the horses were taken from the guns to water, and the men fell out for a few minutes.

In the meantime the advanced guard turned to the right, and pursued its way along the bank of the canal. It was not aware that the main body had halted, as it was hidden by a belt of trees that lined the canal. A vedette far on the left flank brought in the intelligence that the enemy were in force in front, on the flank, and stretching for more than a mile opposite the road the advanced guard had passed over, but they were concealed in the topes* that grew so thickly around Nugeena.

The guard was now in considerable danger, as the column had not yet crossed; but the news set the force into rapid motion, and, with such practised soldiers, a few minutes only were required to place it in line of battle. Then the enemy's guns opened, but they opened only to give points of attack to the different regiments moving swiftly on. It was now discovered that a heavy battery actually commanded the bridge, and that the rebels had lost another of the many chances offered by the fortune of war of inflicting on us serious loss. It was said they were late in taking up their position, and the General earlier in the field than could have been expected; which may have been the case, as he had

* Groves of trees.

already marched some fourteen miles. It is, however, a fact that, though they did often foolishly desperate acts, they still more frequently failed to seize the most favourable opportunities.

Rapidity of movement was now economy of life, and each regiment swept on to its attack with a speed that left the Artillery little time for action, and dispersed the rebel force as chaff before a high wind.

Short as this action was, it was sufficiently fatal to the men of Rohilcund. More than a thousand of them were killed in the field, all their guns were taken, the city was occupied, and none dared thenceforth openly to dispute the march of "the Avenger."

The column quickly advanced on Mooradabad, which the rebels as hastily evacuated. Nearly all the local leaders of influence were captured in that city, and the chief of them was at once shot, to prevent the possibility of a rescue. The next day the bodies of the others swung on a long gibbet in the centre of the beautiful little cantonment they had so desolated.

As the force moved on, the enemy abandoned the forts on its left, and the fords of the river on its right; and thus relieved the Doab from the pressure the presence of the mutineers had kept up on our side, while the fugitives went flocking in thousands to Bareilly.

In vain Kahn Bahadoor Khan sent out a General to check the progress of the column. The latter made a display with his cavalry, but the Brigadier-General's Irregulars, supported by a squadron of Dragoon Guards, stole round to his flank, then charged, and he was driven in at full gallop, with the loss of all his guns, and it is said of his own life.

Already the Commander-in-chief was nearing the capital, and the short space between the approaching columns was densely occupied by those whose black deeds were beyond the pale of forgiveness. The traitor Khan now trembled for his existence, notwithstanding the countenance and support of that determined miscreant the Lucknow Mouloie, and of that infamous monster the Nana, who is reported to have said to the cowering chief, "It is as well to be drowned with a foot of water over your head as with an inch." It was not water, however, that was to finish the career of the Khan; he was destined to be hanged, and although he managed for years to evade this fate, yet the day came when he died on a gibbet in the capital he had ruled—boasting, when he saw there was no hope of mercy, of his own excesses, and of the number of Kaffirs his orders had consigned to Jehannum.

It was in vain that the Brigadier-General strove to obtain intelligence of his Excellency's movements. Messenger after messenger was despatched with promises of a high reward if one of them succeeded in bringing back a reply to the little piece of paper rolled up in a quill they were given to carry—but no reply came. The country actually swarmed with the enemy's cavalry. The Brigadier-General, confident in his own force, dashed straight at the town, and on the day following that when Sir Colin defeated Khan Bahadoor Khan, some seven miles from Bareilly, the Roorkee Field Force, pushing back all opposition, entered the city, and fighting its way through the streets, gained the centre, and there occupied and barricaded the principal buildings.

Then the shells from the other column fell crashing through the roofs of these houses, so that the forces actually came in contact before their proximity could be ascertained. Three men of the

Rifles passed over the deserted streets till they emerged at the opposite end of the town, where they beheld, in long lines of tents, the immense array of his Excellency's force. The junction was then complete, but the nest of great traitors was gone; the Nana, the Khan, and the Mouloie —all had fled; and the torrent pent up between the approaching columns had poured round the flank of the Chief, and inundated his rear.

The difficulty was to deal with the numerous horsemen that formed the chief strength of the revolted province, and while his Excellency was operating against Bareilly, they were threatening the posts along the line of his communication, had recaptured Shahjehanpore, and were shelling the garrison which had taken refuge in the gaol.

The Roorkee Field Force was broken up, and the Brigadier-General, with his staff, was appointed to one of still greater strength, to march as quickly as possible to the relief of this garrison.

The atmosphere was now heated to the temperature of a burning furnace—a heat those only can understand who have experienced it. I will not dwell on a subject Mr. Russell's graphic pen has described, who then learned, in common with the newly arrived soldiers, what the withering effects of a hot weather campaign in India really are.

The relief was effected, and Shahjehanpore occupied; but the enemy assembled in great masses in front of the town, and his numerous cavalry rode freely over the country. More than once he attacked the position, and a portion of his horse actually burst into the cantonment through the force drawn out, and were cut up or dispersed in the rear.

After Sir Colin had completed the arrangements for the occupation of Rohilcund, he passed through Shahjehanpore with a strong escort, remaining there a few days. He had scarcely arrived when the Mouloie, who commanded the opposing forces, and was more soldier than priest, attacked him. One shot nearly finished his career, passing between him and the now celebrated chief of the staff.

The greater portion of the escort was left with the Brigadier-General, who was further reinforced by a brigade of Punjab troops, under a tried and able leader, and he received orders to drive the rebels through Mahumdee back into the Terai.

The sun rose, on the morning of the 24th May, on the glittering line with which the General swept the country. No power in Asia could for a moment, on such a plain, have borne the shock of such a force, and the enemy, like a swarm of bees buzzing thickly before and around the flanks, vanished from its front.

The sun did what the rebels could not do—it filled the hospitals, and strewed the rear with dead. Mahumdee was taken, the forts destroyed, and the enemy scattered; so the General withdrew to Shahjehanpore, the Field Force was broken up, and the troops retired into quarters from the deadly sun, now acting with a force that even the most seasoned could not withstand.

CHAPTER VII.

Tragedies at Shahjehanpore—Indian Travelling in Hot Weather—Intermittent Fever—Rewarding on Compulsion—Valour of the Seikhs—Entrance into the Punjab—Region of Hills—A Change for the Better.

A MILITARY body on active service requires a much more extensive staff than the same troops in quarters. When the Field Force, therefore, returned it was at once broken up, and my husband was at liberty to take up the appointment to which he had been nominated. But was it advisable? The heat was appalling, the distance more than a thousand miles.

Under other circumstances such a journey would not have been undertaken; now the temptation was irresistible. The imagination revelled amid cool breezes on the snowy heights near the fairy region of Cashmere, and I received an intimation that Captain M. would immediately commence his return. On his way back, as well as on the march from Hurdwan, he passed through three ruined cantonments of no ordinary beauty. Each had its tragic story, and each presented to us a type of the senseless and wanton destruction that marked the career of the mutineers. Of these the most tragic and the most beautiful was that of Shahjehanpore.

The station lay behind the city, both standing on a tongue of land between two rivers, the latter occupying the spot where the waters of these streams met. A pretty church had been erected in the centre of the ground allotted to the military. It was a ruin, memorable for one of the most bloodthirsty deeds of this miserable revolt.

From Mooradabad the English rode to Meerut; from Bareilly many got away to Nynee-tal, but from Shahjehanpore there was no escape.

It was in that church, when the victims were assembled to worship God, that the crime was perpetrated. It was on His altar that the blood of His people fell. Could human nature look unmoved on such a spot? Is it surprising that both the Governor-General and the Commander-in-chief strove in vain to restrain the thirst for vengeance, and that a word for mercy and forgiveness stamped its utterer as a "white pandy?" It was with a savage delight that the Artillery pitched their shells into the deserted city, and many officers with secret satisfaction saw a whole quarter of the town in flames.

I had forwarded the things reserved from the sale of our furniture, many days before my husband's arrival, by that useful institution, the Government bullock vans. Almost immediately after his return we left Meerut on a journey I will long remember, doing our first stage to Delhi on the 8th June, 1858.

The first portion of our journey was performed in gharries, but much the greater part was by *palkee dâk*, that is, borne on the shoulders of Coolies. During the night we travelled, resting, when the sun had risen, at the Travellers' Bungalows. In every country where travelling is the most primitive, it is, at the same time, uncomfortable, expensive, and slow. A change is coming over India, and these miserable journeys will soon be unknown. Some years hence the traveller over the same ground will scarcely be able to realize the wretched way we were compelled to traverse the country from Umballa to Murree.

Up to Umballa the road was complete, and the little pony dragged on the great gharry at a considerable pace; but from this station our real troubles commenced, and the farther north we got the worse and the more insolent the bearers became. I often heard them discussing the great topic of the day, and generally they expressed doubts of our success at Delhi. Their idea was that the empire was still in jeopardy, and, native-like, their rudeness was in proportion to this belief. As I feared being left behind, I directed my palkee to be carried in front. Often it was with difficulty that the relays of bearers could be procured, and the sun would rise before we reached our shelter, and light up the white road and the baked plain with an intolerable glare. When he reached any height, our frail coverings seemed to curl and crack, and his rays struck upon the parched earth with a dazzling reflection, which a person in the strongest health could scarcely endure.

I was grieved to see that my husband's health had suffered severely from the effects of the hot weather campaigns. An intermittent fever and ague seized him with a strong hold. It is often so with soldiers, who, supported by the excitement of a campaign, will suffer more from disease when the work ceases than during the actual operations.

We had done half our journey when I began to doubt the wisdom of having undertaken it at all. Hitherto I had lived in well-cooled bungalows during the hot weather, and I had no idea what I was undertaking until I was embarked in the task. One morning, when day broke, I looked behind for my husband's palkee along the straight monotonous road, which I could trace away to the horizon where it became a dot. Surprised that there was no palkee in sight, I despatched a messenger with a note to learn the cause, and awaited his arrival in a serai. It was hours before my husband came, and then in a native cart. He told me the Coolies had deserted and left his palkee on the road, where it would have been death to remain. He had therefore left it, and taken the opportunity of a passing cart to proceed. Desiring me to follow, he continued his way to Punritsan.

When I entered my palkee, the bearers had vanished, and though I had waited for hours, it was now that they began to eat and to smoke.

When they resumed the journey, the sun was high, and they suffered so much that at every well I was left on the burning highway till they had quenched their thirst. It was near the meridian when I reached the Dâk bungalow; the paint was burnt off the palanquin, and no words can describe the heat, which this morning passed even the endurance of nature, for dense clouds gathering burst into torrents of rain, and the earth trembled beneath the roar of the thunder.

As I expected, I found my husband suffering from an attack of fever, and the doctor, an old friend who came to see us, advised him to proceed with all speed to the hills. When we started that night, I told the bearers that, as the sahib was ill, we must reach Lahore before sun-rise, and for extra speed they should receive double *buksheesh*. At the first stage they were an hour over time, so I refused the reward, and directed them to carry the invalid, who was asleep, beyond the sound of the altercation. The new Coolies refused to proceed until the old ones had received the promised *buksheesh*, and they all sat down in a circle, and passed round the hubble-bubble, whilst I in despair could see the torches of the other palkee in the distance as it was borne away. A native wearing the Government badge passed, and I asked his assistance, but he replied that these people had become so independent since the mutiny, that my only plan was to give the sum they demanded, which I was compelled to do.

On this tiresome journey we crossed the Sutledge, the Ravee, the Beas, the Chenab, and the Jhelum, the five rivers which give their combined name to the province.* Between the two last lies the plain where the Seikhs made their final stand against the British. My husband, who had been present in the battle, pointed out the ground where the power of this warlike sect had been broken under the walls of Goojerat. The difference between the fighting qualities of the Seikhs and the Bengal Sepoys was strikingly displayed in the campaigns of the Sutledge and Punjab, and those of the mutiny. The best contested actions fought in India were on these fields. There was something noble in the fair and open ground taken by the old Kalsa army. They massed their troops and came boldly into the clear plains, inviting pitched battles; and when beaten, after several of

* Punjab, or Five Rivers.

the bloodiest encounters since Waterloo, they surrendered. Like Cromwell's Ironsides on the return of Charles II., they took to honest agriculture, leaving the victorious army staggered by their losses, and full of admiration for the prowess of their foes.

I woke in the night, after I had crossed the field of Goojerat, from a dream that I was in a goodly ship on my passage home. The ripple of water and the splash of oars sounded in my ears. I looked abroad over a wide expanse of sea, and I thought my dream was true; but I was only on the mighty stream that drains the valley of Cashmere—the great and rapid Jhelum. I was on the route of the armies that, from time immemorial, had thus passed to the conquest of India. It was here that Porus had vainly attempted to stop the march of Alexander; and during the many centuries that had since elapsed, several conquerors had pursued the same path, till our own great nation had turned the tide in the opposite direction, and the victorious armies now moved from the plains of Hindostan.

Some years before, Sir Walter Gilbert lost many of his camp followers while fording this stream in his quick pursuit of the Afghan and Punjab forces, when he was accompanied by the Rifles, in which my husband was then a lieutenant.

Hitherto this journey had been over a country without a hill, except where the land rose beyond the Jhelum, and was broken by the most extraordinary ruts and chasms. It seemed as if the surface had been level, and heavy rains had torn it up, leaving it intersected, after a series of deluges, with innumerable gigantic water-courses. The old road from the town of Jhelum led for some thirty miles through one of these passes, and close to its entrance is situated one of those forts of gigantic walls which are so often seen in the Mahratta country. This was the Bukralla Pass, and the Fort of Rotas.

Now I was about to enter the region of hills where my imagination had not ceased to dwell, the thought of which had sustained me during that fatiguing time, and which was to reward me for all the trials of that fearful road.

From the bungalow at Rawul-Pindee, I looked up to the dark line of mountains where the station stood; and it was with an indescribable pleasure that I entered the palkee for the last time. There was a change in the dress and appearance of the bearers—even the mode of carrying the palanquin was different. I saw this at a glance—I felt it in the motion, and I heard it in the grunts by which the bearers relieve the monotony of their toilsome stage.

CHAPTER VIII.

A Bungalow in the Hills—Sanatorium at Murree—Firing Cannon at a Target—Mountainous Scenery—Military Command of the Station—Expensive Necessaries—Effects of a Damp Cloud—Attack of Malignant Cholera—Sir John Lawrence endeavours to check the Pestilence—Value of Sanatoriums—Attempts at Amusement—Winter on the Mountains—Last Days at Murree.

I AWOKE as my bearers placed my palkee under the verandah of the Trête Dâk bungalow, and I felt that I was in a different atmosphere.

The bungalow stood on a projection in the centre of a long valley, in which I could trace the road winding among the trees in the hollows, and coming out in the bare sides of the projections, till it was lost beyond the tower* at the top, with nothing but the clear sky behind it. The sides of this valley low down were cut in terraces, like flights of steps, all glittering with an inundation of water. These were rice-fields; cottages were grouped here and there in the queerest and most improbable places, standing out like large boulders from the rocky sides of the mountain. A stream ran rapidly down the dark hollow beneath, and circled round the projection where I stood. The road I had come up was cut along a precipice down to the stream, which it crossed by a romantic bridge, and both it and the water were lost in the black gorge far below. The mountains reared their majestic sides so near that I could not see their tops. Here they were wooded, there green with grass, and anon piled up with frowning rocks. Everything was changed around me—the vegetation, the aspect of Nature, and the climate.

Seldom have I felt happier than when borne up this hill to the picturesque station of Murree. I regarded the scene as one regards a prize he has toiled hard to gain. Gurgling streams came sparkling down the slopes, and murmured along with a sound sweeter than music to my ear. Imagination carried me back to the days of my childhood; and in fancy I was again in an English dell, with the trickling water rolling over the mossy stones. I could not resist the inclination to walk where the towering mountain gave me shade, or the branches of the forest broke the rays of the sun. This is a proceeding regarded by the bearers as a cabman would regard a fare who insisted upon getting into the street and running after the cab.

I passed a pretty garden, and was gracefully presented with a bouquet of flowers by a little boy. This act augured well for the feeling of the hill people.

As we approached the summit, the hateful sound of cannon rumbled from above, and I could see where the balls struck. The target was placed close by a cutting on the hill side, which marked the course of the road, and we were obliged to send a Cooly to stop the firing until we had passed. The higher we mounted, the more eagerly I looked up for some signs of the station, yet it was long before a house came in sight. The first I saw was built on a peak so high above me, and so abrupt, that I could not believe it was inhabited. Gradually others appeared, filling me with awe at their position; but as I approached their level, they fell into their proper places, and my feelings changed with my own ascent, till I looked down with contempt on the very houses I had looked up to with awe from below. How truly this illustrates the career of many; and probably I might have been inclined to regard my fellow-creatures with the same feelings, unless watched and checked, if my ascent in life had been equally rapid.

The bearers toiled up through a thick wood, and suddenly we came on a handsome level road. We had reached the Mall, and stood in the centre of the station of Murree.

The Sanatorium is elevated more than seven thousand feet above the sea, and is on the high road from Cashmere to the plains of India. It was established on the annexation of the Punjab, and has since continued to be the convalescent depôt for that great province. The Mall passes between and circles round the two peaks bounding the saddle-like ridge where the station stands. The barracks are excellent, and are picturesquely placed near the centre. Considering the short time it has been established, the houses are good, and the roads are excellent.

The bleak winds from the north have left the steep precipices, or *kuds*, as they are called, facing that direction bare of timber; but on the south side the slopes are densely wooded. The Mall winds through the noble pines of the forest, amid whose branches gambol countless monkeys. Small paths lead to houses hidden among the tall straight stems of innumerable pines. Out from the damp and gloomy shade the chief road emerges on the crest, and then the spectator sees the vastness of the Himalayah.

To one thoroughly imbued with the scenery of this region, all other mountains are only hills—those of Scotland would be ruts on a frosty road. The pines struggle up to the crest, and stand erect in defiance of the storm, their branches torn, and here and there their trunks blasted by lightning. The Mall winds round the peak, passing the best houses of the station. The bazaar lies below the barracks, and a pretty church stands in a hollow close by, through which the road leads to Cashmere.

The military command is limited to two years, and a subordinate, termed a "station staff," is detailed for the same period. The duty officers remain during the season, or hot weather, as well as nearly all the men (selected by the doctors from the European regiments in the province), numbering about four hundred. The command allowance of £20 per month scarcely suffices for the increased expense of every necessary; yet the appointment is eagerly sought, as people pay to go to the hills, and consider the permission an indulgence.

The house we were fortunate enough to secure was rented, unfurnished, at from £100 to £120 per annum. In England it would be considered a very small, very badly built, and very inconvenient cottage. As food is dear, and more clothing necessary, higher wages are demanded by the servants; and those who do not bring their own, find it difficult to get any, and impossible to get good ones. Everything, even water, is carried up the mountain on the backs of men, mules, or camels. Such transport is always dear, no matter what may be the price of labour; and wine, beer, and all English stores are therefore extravagantly high. Some cases of wine sent to us from Calcutta cost little short of two shillings for the carriage of each bottle alone; though I must add that the greater part of this enormous sum was charged by the Ganges Steam Navigation Company for that portion of the transport which ought to have been the cheapest.

We had purchased some articles of furniture, and were beginning to feel settled in our new house, when a dark cloud gathered over the station. The cholera had been raging in Cashmere, and the doctor reported some cases of a suspicious nature that appeared at the depôt.

The dark cloud was a literal fact, as well as a figurative expression, for a column of mist fell over the hill as a pall, penetrating into every house. There it hung like death; stealing around all the contents, and spreading over them a green and unhealthy mould. Shoes left for the night looked in the morning as if taken from a vault with the rot of a year on them. Scarcely a breath stirred the leaves —nothing moved, except the rain that at intervals fell in torrents. The air was without electricity, without wind, and loaded with moisture—we were living in a stagnant cloud.

One day, on my husband's return from the orderly-room, I heard that the dire disease had grasped the depôt. I was amazed as well as horrified to learn that five men, out of the small force, were lying in the dead-house; many more were dying, and cases were rapidly filling the hospital. Was it possible?—could this really be the work of a few hours?

Then commenced one of those trying periods well known in India, and that we may be thankful Providence has made so short. So malignant was the epidemic at this stage, that men attacked could scarcely hope to see the sun go down. Many who rose in what they considered health, slept in their graves before night; and it was shocking to learn that the orderly who had carried a message to the house was buried when next inquired for.

Still the pall hung over us—still the rain came down in heavy sullen showers, and the mist and damp grew around, and entered into our very marrow. I listened eagerly for a peal of thunder. I would have given almost anything to have seen the cloud rent by lightning, and it would have been music to have heard the roar of a tempest tearing up the trees of the forest. I felt as if a net had been thrown over the station, and that noxious and deadly gases had been let loose in the atmosphere. But the most horrid feeling was that of stagnation. How I longed to see nature in commotion!—to see the hand of God raised to deliver us from this scourge!

Every measure holding out a chance of staying the pestilence was adopted, and, fortunately for the poor soldiers, Sir John Lawrence was at the station. This distinguished civil servant, who took the most lively interest in the sufferings of the men, was a constant visitor at the hospital, and cheered by his presence, as well as by his kind words and acts, the stricken and the dying soldiers.

My husband had the satisfaction of knowing that every means the Government could command, every luxury the station could afford, was lavishly supplied. The first step taken was to break up the depôt; and for this purpose a very large house was given over by order of Sir John Lawrence.

The epidemic was singularly partial in its choice of locality. As usual, it commenced in the hospital, and there was a detached barrack standing near it that proved almost certain death to sleep in. The men, being invalids, fell an easier prey, but I doubt whether the epidemic ever showed itself on the plains in a more virulent form than here, in a region hitherto considered exempt from such visitations.

Though more than one-sixth of the force were buried before the pestilence left, yet only two of the European residents at the station died. This is often the case in the plains, where it is no uncommon thing to see a number of the soldiers fall victims to cholera, while no other English inhabitant of the cantonment is attacked.

This was the first appearance of cholera at any of the sanitary stations, but these depôts have not, as yet, proved their salubrity. Statistics are liable to error in the results they convey, still there is much point in the fact that not one of these establishments on the peaks of the Himalayah stands at the head of the list of the comparative healthiness of Indian stations. Rawul-Pindee has recorded fewer deaths and a smaller sick-list from an equal number of soldiers than any of these. It may be said that invalids are quartered at the Sanatoria, yet there are hill stations with entire regiments, as at Kussowlie and Dugshai, which are not found to be so healthy as Umballa or Rawul-Pindee.

After the Punjab war my husband's battalion was quartered at Subathoo and Kussowlie, close to

Simla, where the men suffered much from sickness. It may be that the seeds of disease were sown in the campaign, during which they marched nearly all the way from Kurrachee to Peshawur, starting at the end of one hot season, and not arriving till the next was well advanced. The soldiers were pleased to find themselves again in the plains; and, from what I could gather, I conclude that they like these hill stations as a change for a short period, but not as a quarter for a long period.

The value of these Sanatoria, however, is not to be estimated by their comparative salubrity. To the heat-exhausted resident of the cantonment below, the cool and invigorating air must be beneficial; nor is this change confined to the atmosphere. After the monotonous wards of an hospital, with its walled enclosure, without a flower—after the interminable flat, with its endless crops and villages—the eye rests with an indescribable relief on the vast mountains, and their wild and tangled vegetation.

Though it was the poor soldiers and the Natives in the bazaar who died, yet few of the people in Murree escaped without an attack of illness. The atmosphere had during this time a power of seizing on any weakness or aggravating any complaint to which a person was liable. I was pained to see how much Colonel M.'s* constitution had been affected by exposure in the campaigns, and it was with considerable dread I observed his constant attendance in a spot where the plague seemed to have developed all its venom. I could not utter a word of objection to visits to the hospital and barrack-rooms, for no duty could be more clear. Still his health had been so undermined that the risk he ran was much increased, and so was my anxiety.

I had lost faith, after this sad introduction to the command, in the restorative power of the climate of Murree, and I felt that a total change of scene was required, as well as of climate. I strongly urged, therefore, a return to Europe. My husband was loath to lose the benefits of the appointment it had cost him so much to take up, and the doctors recommended him to wait and try the effects of the cold season.

The weather that followed in the autumn was charming in the extreme, and the atmosphere

* My husband had now attained the brevet rank of Lieutenant-Colonel.

assumed the purity and the brilliancy of an Italian sky. Then the station became the gayest, the days were enlivened by pic-nics, and many evenings with pleasant little dances. One of these pic-nics was planned on a large scale, for the soldiers who were to compete for prizes in athletic exercises. The only level ground, about two miles distant, called Topah, or the "Flat," was chosen. When on my way there, I inquired why a number of men I passed were returning. I was informed that the camel, on whose back the delicacies had been packed, had fallen down the *Kud*. This was a disastrous end for the plum-pudding and pies I had been manufacturing for days; and not even the young soldiers, for whom they were intended, could have grieved more than myself over the sad loss.

Notwithstanding these little efforts at amusement, the station could not easily shake off the effects of the recent fatal visitation, and soon the people began to hurry back to their work on the plains. One by one, and family by family, they disappeared, and we were left by degrees almost alone on the desolate mountain, amid the forsaken houses.

As the season progressed the air became extremely rare, and even difficult to breathe—icicles formed and snow fell. We watched the "Black Forest" mountain that faced our window, and gave the earliest symptom of approaching winter. A grey sprinkling first appeared, streaked more boldly in white lines on the dark colouring of the tree tops. Perceptibly it spread, until a great field of snow coldly glittered on this high elevation, ten thousand feet above the sea. Then it stole down the sides; lower peaks showed similar signs; we were scarcely conscious that our own hill was streaked in the same manner with white. The vales below put on the spotless mantle, and the country around was clad by degrees in an icy covering. The snow thickened on the roads, the forest bent under its weight, individual trees sparkled as if hung with diamonds, and great festoons of icicles were suspended from the roofs.

Now I saw hoary winter for the first time. In England we see boisterous winter—gloomy, sullen, and wet—but never this. The sun shone as brightly as before, the whole landscape glittered in a manner not to be described, and all the gems in the world, grouped into one mass, could not equal the brilliancy of a single tree, when its icy coat was lighted into dazzling brightness by the rays of the sun. Could anyone believe this to be India?—was it not rather Siberia or Spitzbergen?

The houses, built for summer, not for winter, were scarcely habitable, and whole trunks of trees were insufficient to give heat to a room beyond a few feet from the fire. Here was a Christmas region for Anglo-Indians to revel in! and on Christmas Day all who remained at Murree dined together.

That night, when we regained our home, a work of no small difficulty in such weather, a bugle rang out the alarm. My heart sank at the sound, and the horrors that had followed it on the 10th May passed like phantoms before my mind. As I looked in the direction of the barracks, whither my husband had hurried, a bright glare told that a portion of the buildings was on fire. The relief was inexpressible when I learnt that it arose from a simple cause. The men had been heaping up a Christmas fire, till the beams of the roof, which projected into the flue, caught the flame, and the shingles were soon in a blaze. The Seikhs, who were quartered in an adjoining building, were alarmed at the thought of being suspected, and none were more active than they in extinguishing the flames.

I wonder if there is any station in India on which a shade from the great nightmare that passed over thel and—the Mutiny—has not fallen. Even Murree, secluded in the hills, has its own tale. The Paharrees* had assembled, to attack the station, in the thick forest below, and they advanced through this cover against some houses lying on the outskirts. They were met and defeated by a few armed residents and invalid soldiers, and in this affair some men were killed and others taken and hanged.

The doctor, who had waited to see the effects of this period, now strongly recommended my husband to proceed to England; and this was confirmed by a Board, and sanctioned by the Commander-in-chief.

I was sorry to leave without visiting Cashmere, as I had heard much of the beauty of that romantic valley. An interdict had been placed on the district, arising from the universal cause of agitation and strife. It is within nine days' journey

* Hill-men.

by narrow precipitous paths in a dandy, a conveyance consisting of a blanket slung on a pole.

A depôt had been established at Murree for the sale of its shawls, but the prices were high, and the shop was only open during the summer.

Snakes and scorpions are numerous at Murree, and in the winter bears and hyenas often enter the station. There were pheasants and jungle-fowl in the wood, and, at the foot of the hills, black partridge, hares, and pea-fowl. Tigers have been fatal, and a predecessor in the command was killed by one. There are some good *parseer* in the streams, a fish that attains a large size, and readily takes a fly.

America has extended her mission to this region, and a few of its members were studying the dialects before penetrating into Central Asia. The Dâk bungalows throughout India afford proof of the usefulness of this Moravian Mission, for the traveller will find in each a neat case of well-assorted religious works. We obtained from this source, to which I had subscribed a small sum, many excellent books of travels and history at a low price, published at Philadelphia.

Perhaps my last act at Murree was to write a

letter of apology under circumstances that illustrate the difficulty of comprehending the working of the native mind. All the water for the house had to be carried by a bheestie* up a steep path from a well far down the hill-side. To save him this toil, we bought a bullock with the necessary skins. No sooner did the bheestie see it, than, with tears in his eyes, he begged to be left to his work, and not compelled to adopt a *new way*; adding, that he would double the quantity if required. I explained that it was solely for *his* benefit the purchase had been made, but he was not happy till the animal had been expelled. The bullock then roamed at pleasure over the station, as I found it impossible to keep it confined to our compound. This led to complaints from people whose gardens had been devoured, and caused me much embarrassment, as I objected to kill the offender, and I was otherwise unable to get rid of it. Unless some one has eaten it, it may be walking about the station still.

* A water-carrier.

CHAPTER IX.

Proceedings against the Mutineers at the Cantonment of Jhelum—A Comfortable House—Visit to the Fort of Moultan—Designs of the Mutineers—Their Excesses—Embark on Board the Steamer *Havelock*—The Indian Navy—Delicate Fish—Arrival at Kurrachee—The Cantonments.

I LEFT Murree on the 31st December, 1858, a few days before my husband was ready, as it was feared that a fall of snow might shut up the road, and I remained at the house of a friend at Rawul-Pindee till he had finished his business. Our baggage had been forwarded to Jhelum, whither we followed almost immediately after.

The cantonment of Jhelum escaped ruin, as the mutineers had not held it while in open rebellion, though it was the scene of one of the fiercest struggles of the mutiny. A portion of the 24th, under Colonel Ellis, with some guns, were sent to disarm the Native troops. The Sepoys took to their huts, and from this cover opened a heavy fire upon the English soldiers. When driven from their shelter, they fell back on another line, and the fighting continued among the houses all the day, with heavy loss of life. Before the Natives were expelled, the Colonel, with scores of his men, had fallen.

Not far from this spot, so near, indeed, as to be within sound of the cannon, is situated another field, on the banks of the Jhelum. Only a few years had elapsed since the soldiers of this regiment lay there dead in hundreds. Seldom, indeed, even in British fights, had a battalion of our army suffered to a like extent, for half the officers engaged were killed, and nearly all of the other half were wounded; while more than five hundred wearing the uniform of the corps lay strewn on the field of Chillianwallah. It will be long ere this field is forgotten in the annals of the 24th.

We found that the Deputy-Commissioner had prepared two boats for our passage down the stream. These large, flat-bottomed craft are engaged by measurement, and then fitted with a mat house, according to the purse and fancy of the traveller. One was for ourselves, the other for our servants. The mat-house erected on that for us had a sitting-room, a bed-room, and a bath-room; the other, a kitchen, and a servant's room. Stock is laid in as for a voyage, and the boats float down the broad stream day after day, mooring, or *lagowing*, as it is termed, during the night. Heavy clouds hung over the hills, and it was raining fast when we started. At night the river rose, and before daylight the bank where we moored was inundated, and we were swept down the strong flood like chips in a current. As we dashed along in the grey light of early dawn, we saw the people of a village working hard to remove their property. Masses of the bank were tumbling down, and the interiors of some of the houses were exposed to view. How unpleasant must be a residence in a situation so precarious!

The salt ranges to the right, though a mine of wealth to the Government, looked barren and desolate. From these mines—of course a Government monopoly, as is all salt in the country—the supply is extracted for the inhabitants of this portion of India; and it can be traced a vast distance over the provinces, till it reaches a boundary line where that from the sea comes into competition. A few miles to the left lay the celebrated battle-ground of Chillianwallah, with the heights Shere Sing had held rising abruptly, and showing signs that the river had once flowed at their feet, though now some two or three miles from its bed.* Beyond the height, near a village which has given its name to the field, a tall column rises from the spot where a legion of England's finest soldiers lie buried—the fatal, and almost the only result of that disastrous action.

When darkness settled on the river, we lagowed and walked on shore, then retired to rest, and started again at daylight. The boatmen do not trouble themselves much by rowing, the water rolling on between three and four miles an hour, and often rushing down a rapid at far greater speed. Thus we generally accomplished some fifty miles in the day. It occasionally blew fresh across the stream,

* The Seikhs fought with these precipices and this river in their rear, and had Lord Gough succeeded in his plan, which was only frustrated by a wise movement on the part of his adversary, nothing more would have been heard of the Khalsa army.

and then we were driven against the bank, our boat being as unmanageable as that of a school-boy. The crews, quite satisfied, would go on shore and gather sticks to prepare their dinners, and no goading of ours had any effect. We proceeded in this manner for days, with little to interest us save the flights of birds, and the drowsy crocodiles basking in the sun.

We passed into the Chenab, and as the stream from the junction continues to be called by that name, the greater river is lost in the lesser. Then we received the waters of the Ravee, and next day reached Moultan, the highest spot connected with the sea by steam.

The arrival and departure of vessels is uncertain, and we were compelled to take our chance, though we had tried to obtain information to guide our departure from Murree. Our disappointment was bitter on learning that a steamer had just left, and that it would be days before another arrived.

The cantonment, like every place of importance on this river, is several miles from its banks. The Indus has no regularly cut channel. It courses over a wide expanse to the sea, and all Scinde may be said to be its bed. The heavy splash of its falling banks never ceases, as the winding river, deserting its channel, seeks a new one in the cultivated country. Then the capricious water meets with an impediment, after destroying the villages and fields for hundreds of square miles, and turns back over the course it had vacated, when green with grain, and covered with villages, and goes splash—splash—splash—till it sweeps them all from the face of creation. Nowhere in the neighbourhood will this tyrant allow a town to arise whose foundation is not guaranteed by a rocky charter, against which the river frets and fumes in vain. Sometimes its waters take a strange revenge, as at Tatta, by leaving the city whose prosperity had been connected with its vicinity, isolated in the desert. Such a river in England would require a code of laws, and furnish work for a second Lincoln's Inn, for I believe it to be beyond the power of engineering.

We had no alternative but to remain, and we tried to obtain shelter nearer than the cantonment. My husband, who had landed with this object, returned to shew me a house that he said might answer. When I saw the ruin I thought he must be joking, as it was simply a shell, without roof, doors, or windows. Our boat-houses were made to supply these deficiencies, and the place assumed something of a habitable form. At night, when the lights were extinguished, the wild animals, to whom the place really belonged, came in wonder to ascertain the cause of the strange change. Wolves scratched at the doors, jackals howled outside, and an unknown creature, supposed to be a wild cat, bounded across the room. I arose and dressed to prepare for the arrival of visitors of greater pretensions. As we decided this place would not do, we made a move to secure a substantial shelter in the cantonment, the more so as our gipsy home would have been a still poorer defence against the storm that threatened than against the original inhabitants.

We met with a kind reception from a stranger, who placed a vacant bungalow at our disposal; and it was well that we did not delay, for a cloud of dust swept over the station, followed by rain that inundated the country.

I took much interest in a visit to the fort, as Colonel M. had been present at the siege and capture in 1848–49. The road is pretty, but the site of the fort is now a huge mound, with a mosque standing on the crest, and some of the bomb-proofs that furnished so poor a defence from our shells to the followers of Moolraj. Every trace had disappeared of those towering walls whose triple row had rendered this citadel famous as a place of strength. Punjeet Sing had lost an army before his flag floated from the spot where I stood, and for months the ground around was occupied by the formidable force brought against it by the British, before they became masters of the place.

My husband could scarcely fix the direction of the approaches—although he had seen many a gallant soldier fall in carrying up the sap, and the circumstances of a first campaign remain strongly fixed in the memory—so completely had the fort of Moultan disappeared.

Moultan was the scene of one of those singular outbreaks that for their folly could only have excited the derision of the world, had they not been attended with such fearful tragedies. Two disarmed Native regiments had remained there quietly until scarcely a vestige was left of the revolution except the vast political ruin it had wrought. The soldier had accomplished his work, all but the final chase, leaving to the monster the life of a hunted hare, and every double seemed to be his last. At this stage, late in 1858, these regiments conceived the project of raising anew this monster's head. Had they seen something of the appalling nature of the work they proposed, in the fields of bones whitening in the North West Provinces, the desolation that had fallen on their fair cities, even they might have shrunk from the task. Had they known the hecatombs of their kind that had perished in the vain attempt—the number of princes and peasants that had died on the gallows, victims to their ignorance of England and the English—they must have drawn back, if rational men, or beings gifted with the capacity of learning from experience. Failing this knowledge, it is strange that instinct should not have told them the attempt was certain to be at once fatal to themselves.

A battery of the Royal Artillery, the 1st Bombay Fusiliers, and an Irregular Cavalry regiment were quartered in the barracks. The plan was to rush into the rooms of the infantry soldiers while the men lay drowsily on their beds during the heat, to seize on their arms, and to possess themselves of the guns. They were persuaded that the cavalry were more likely to act with than against them; and they hoped, after cutting to pieces the Europeans in the station, to form a complete and powerful brigade, with which they could march straight against Lahore.

An eye-witness informed me that just before the mid-day gun—the appointed signal—he heard some sinister rumours in the bazaar that induced him to proceed towards the European lines. When it was fired he saw the Sepoys, armed with every weapon they could appropriate—and the number, in spite of precautions, was considerable—rush with loud cries on the barracks of the Fusiliers.

A moment like this comprises years of life. When fortune or ruin rests on one of the horses speeding together to the winning-post, the person whose interest is involved may experience a painful excitement, but what can that be compared to this?—life and all being the stake at issue. The head of the column was entering the verandah; already the sticks and swords were raised to strike, when it was thrown back like a surging wave on a rock-bound coast, and from every window streamed a fire that scattered to all points the Native host.

That the soldiers alone should have been prepared, is another instance that England owes much to their vigilance. So completely was the Punjab taken by surprise, that it is asserted the order from the Chief Commissioner to re-arm these regiments was actually at the time in the station.

The Adjutant of the Fusiliers was met and murdered, and the bands of the Sepoys carried terror and consternation wherever they spread. People living a short way off had to fly for their lives, and all hung in suspense till the conduct of the Cavalry was decided. This regiment was quickly mounted and drawn up under its officers, who decided for them if they ever did waver. Many of the Sepoys died under the sabres of the Sowars, perhaps some of them before they recovered from their astonishment at the hand that administered the blow. The two regiments perished to a man! The country became a large grave; and the world would have looked on aghast at the spectacle, had not the enormous crimes, sufferings, and death involved in the revolt accustomed it to such scenes.

A few telegrams and letters copied from the Indian into the English newspapers was all the notice accorded to a mutiny more sanguinary than that of Barrackpore, more fatal than that of Vellore, which have furnished pages for history and matter for generations to discuss.

The magnitude of events may fairly be judged by the notice accorded to each act. A battle in the later wars of Napoleon, where ten thousand soldiers fell, is treated as an affair of advanced guards, and the extent of the great uprising in India may be estimated by the manner in which the inundation dwarfed heights nature intended for mountains. So this business, in which, a few weeks before, hundreds upon hundreds of men had perished, was almost lost in the tragic acts that so thickly preceded it.

We embarked in the steamer *Havelock*, one of the Honourable Company's boats, where the cabins are few and small, the ladies only sleeping in them, the gentlemen always, when afloat on the coast or on the rivers of India, making a bed for themselves under the awning on deck. The run is made in daylight, and with great care, for, in a river such as I have described, a vessel may be unable to get down a channel she had a few hours before come up. Miles of sand-banks, rising just above the water, occupy the centre of its bed, and it is most difficult to tell through which channel the main body flows. When the snows of the Himalayah, in the hottest months, melt, the tide of the Indus sweeps over these sand-banks, and occupies the whole channel, till the water is almost on a level with the bank, and the traveller in mid-channel sees nothing but a boundless sea in swift motion around him.

With all their care, the steamers often ground, and one morning, when at breakfast—hot tea, poached eggs, and savoury stews distributed—the steamer struck with such violence that we were thrown down in a row on each side of the table, and the tea, crockery, and eggs fell in showers over us; one gentleman only, whose chair was supported by an iron stanchion, remaining a spectator of our fall.

The Indian Navy, with a noble confidence in human nature, make it the interest of the captains of these boats to be as long as possible on the passage, a principal portion of the pay of these gentlemen being derived from a contract for the supply of the passengers with food, by the day, instead of by the passage.

The day after our departure we reached the Punjab, as the five streams are termed, from where the Sutledge joins, to their junction with the Indus at Mittancote. There is no stream of any importance that flows into the Indus from Mittancote to the sea. In fact, the country below that town is a thirsty desert, except along the banks of the river, which supplies the arid soil with water. The river, therefore, loses greatly in its course to the sea; the body of water at Mittancote being much greater than at Zatta. To me the country had a wretched aspect. The distant hills were low, tame, and barren, the banks level and monotonous, the mud houses mere hovels, the stretches of bare sand interminable, or covered with a low green shrub. Sukkur, with the island fort of Bukkur and the singular town of Roorree, with its strange rocks, forms the only spot of beauty. The river has here burst through a range of hills, and these buildings are, perhaps, the most secure from attack on the side towards the sea. After taking in cargo we started again. Among the passengers was a Scindian convict, who had murdered his wife, a crime prevalent in the country, and one the magistrates found it difficult to deal with, as the husband, regarding the English law as a most unjustifiable interference with his right, compelled the wife to hang herself.

We found a "flat," full of passengers, waiting at Kotree to be towed to Kurrachee. Kotree is the terminus of the Scinde Railway. This railway connects the port at Kurrachee with the Indus at Kotree. It was still unfinished.

I was sorry to leave the river without tasting the celebrated *pulla*, a fish said to be most delicate, captured in great numbers, during the season, by men who float down the stream on chatties,* with a triangular net at the end of a pole. The fish, heading up the stream, strike against the net, are caught, and deposited in the chatty. The expertness of these fishers on their chatties, borne on the rapid and most dangerous stream, surprises the lookers-on.

When we got out to sea, the salt water mixing with the fresh in the boilers checked the power of generating steam to a degree I had no idea of, and it was not till the fresh water had been expended that the vessel attained her due speed.

I was charmed once more to see the blue ocean—

* Red earthen jars.

those only can tell how much, who have been encompassed with the dangers that surrounded me hundreds of miles from its shore, and it was with the sea I had always associated safety and the power of my country.

A few hours' steaming brought us from the mouth of the river to the harbour of Kurrachee.

Kurrachee lies to the left of a low line of barren and arid hills, offshoots of the great chains of Central Asia, which attain to their highest grandeur in the vast Himalayah. The country around is a dreary plain of sand, broken by white hillocks, drifted in long ridges. The harbour is formed by a headland, the last promontory of the mountains, called Minora Point. The elevation is a few hundred feet, falling precipitously into the sea where the water attains its greatest depth. From Minora a dreary waste of mud and sand is seen, with a few rocks, near the entrance of the harbour, standing up like ships at sea. At the full the tide invades the desert, and the white sand sparkles in bright contrast with the blue water, but at the ebb the reaches of mud seem endless. The harbour is safe, but there is a bar at the entrance which excludes vessels of very large size. Its left side is formed by a *bundur*, built by Sir Charles Napier, which runs from the town for a considerable distance, connecting it with an island nearly opposite Minora, and on the right side, looking seaward, is Minora and its spit. The town, whose wretched hovels are in keeping with the miserable country, stands at the head of the harbour, on *débris* rising out of the mud, a mere fishing village, for fish abound in these waters.

The cantonment is three miles inland, and is rapidly assuming the dimensions of a city. The clear judgment of Sir Charles Napier foresaw the destiny of the place, and, perhaps, never before had the eye of a founder of a commercial emporium looked on a more uninviting site. Yet Kurrachee is destined to a great future, indeed, to a rivalry with the chief ports of trade; and if the harbour does not fill up, it requires little spirit of prophecy to foretell that a second Bombay will arise at this outlet of the Indus.

Colonel M. had, some years before, been quartered in the cantonment, and had many times passed up and down the Indus. Then no ship was seen at the port except war-steamers with regiments, or with the mails. Now the harbour was crowded with vessels; but, all the way down, the banks that appeared to me so dreary, shewed signs to him of a rapid advance. The mountain tribes begin to learn that there is more to be obtained by commerce than by war. They have already been taught that little is gained, and that often much is lost, by their inroads into our territory, while, by entering into commercial relations with us, they find a ready market for articles they had before looked upon as valueless. Nowhere in the world are the exports increasing with greater speed. The linseed, grain, and flax of the Punjab are only a portion of the vast trade destined to float down the Indus. Wool has become a staple, and no doubt the pastoral tribes will add to this export skins, tallow, and all the produce of stock, and of the wealth that has its origin in grass.

CHAPTER X.

On Board the *Eastern Monarch* bound for England—St. Helena and Longwood—Betting—Care of the Indian Government for its Invalided Soldiers—The *Eastern Monarch* in the Channel—Steering for Portsmouth—The Ship on Fire and Laden with Saltpetre—Terrible Scenes—My Escape—Dreadful Conflagration—The Soldiers Saved—The Ship totally destroyed—My Arrival at Portsmouth—Reach London in the Race Week, without Luggage of any kind.

THE invalids, who had left the Punjab long before us, were awaiting the arrival of a ship taken at Bombay for their conveyance home. This vessel, called the *Eastern Monarch*, was said to be the finest merchant-ship afloat, and we hoped to obtain a passage in her, there being little chance of securing one for a lady by the overland route, as the cabins in these steamers were engaged for several mails.

When the *Eastern Monarch* was signalled, Colonel M. proceeded to her anchorage outside the harbour, as she drew too much water for the bar. He had a race out to secure a cabin, and the following day we embarked with the troops in a small steamer. The ship lay at anchor without a motion, while the steamer was pitching and rolling in the swell, and she dare not go alongside; we were, therefore, transferred by boats, a most unpleasant operation, and not without danger, as one of the boats was sunk and the occupants nearly drowned.

I was charmed when I stood on the deck of the noble *Eastern Monarch*, calmly riding to her anchor, while the little steamer rolled heavily, and the pattama she had towed out full of soldiers was pitching frightfully, and grinding itself to pieces against the ship's sides.

On the evening of the 22nd of February, 1859, the vessel dropped her topsails, and stood out to sea, and I well remember the chorus that rose from many happy hearts as the dreary shores of Beloochistan faded away:

> "Oh! stay, stay, stay"—"No, no—no, no.
> For the sails are spread, and away we go,
> And now we're bound for England, ho!"

Light winds baffled us during the first part of the voyage, and while we lay on the water like a log, we saw the steamer as she crossed swiftly to Aden with some of our fellow-passengers of the *Havelock* on board. The wind freshened after crossing the Line, and we doubled the Cape in beautiful weather on the 8th of April. Ten days more brought us to St. Helena. A few hours after a passenger ship from Calcutta had secured every means of conveyance to Longwood and Napoleon's Tomb. I had then either to walk or give up the idea of visiting these celebrated spots. The road leads along the barren hill side from the deep gully where Jamestown nestles, but as it approaches the top it becomes wooded, and opens a vast prospect of the sea. Before I gained the summit I found the difficulty of the task I had undertaken on a bright day in a tropical climate, but the glorious trade-wind came blowing freshly over the hill when I arrived at the top.

The house once occupied by Napoleon stands on a grassy plateau ventilated by the perpetual breezes of the South-east Trade, and looks down on the stream of ships that flow by on their passage to Europe and North America.

The French had charge, and were collecting materials for the repair of the house, then in a most dilapidated state. The situation is healthy, and not wanting in beauty.

At the foot of one of the abrupt hollows of this lonely and precipitous island, we entered the tomb which once contained all that remained of the great emperor. The vegetation at this spot—for St. Helena—is considerable, but my husband looked with surprise at the renowned willow, the venerated parent of some slips brought by French emigrants to New Zealand, where they had grown into great trees, under whose luxuriant shade he had often bathed in a mountain-stream running into the lovely harbour of Akaroa.

While I write, the bare mountain heights of St. Helena again tower above me. Again its batteries frown on the ship that carries me, and crowds gaze down from the Artillery barracks perched on the rocky summit over the town; but now a change has been effected at Longwood, which has resumed the same habitable shape as when occupied by the mighty genius who there fretted out his life. No more the profane foot of the English traveller shall desecrate the tomb where the great warrior lay, for the French have erected a solid arch of masonry to cover the sacred soil.

On our return we found the captain at the hotel, anxious to get to sea, as the arrival of two such fine ships had roused the innate love of the English for a fair bet, and the people of St. Helena were laying heavy stakes on the arrival in England first of the *Agamemnon* or the *Eastern Monarch*. We had seen the *Agamemnon* get under way, and with surprising speed spread a cloud of canvas to the breeze; but though it was late that night when the *Eastern Monarch* started, we passed her about half way to Ascension.

The only bad weather we experienced was off the Azores, and there would have been little to cloud the monotonous smoothness of the voyage, had it not been for the frequent deaths among our poor invalid soldiers.

The Indian Government has dealt most liberally with its disabled and worn-out troops, in its last act, before it turns them on the wide world. The finest ships that can be procured—the most ample space, light, and ventilation—the best medical attendance, comforts, and even luxuries, are amply supplied. What a pity it is that the lavish expenditure stops here, and the man on whom such care has been bestowed should be found shortly afterwards starving in the streets of London! There were many debilitated by the climate, whose constitution could not be renewed, and they sank by degrees and died, some victims to their own intemperance, but others, alas! to the year too long in India. Men in the last stages of disease are often put on board to give the only chance of recovery, though the doctors have scarcely a hope; but they humour their patients, who are to a certainty, when left behind, left, as they feel and know, to die. Thus we had at sea men destined to a grave in the Southern Ocean, and seventeen were buried before we reached the Cape.

As we neared the Channel, the *Eastern Monarch*, always clean and beautiful, began to glow bright with French polish and paint. The scraping, holystoning, and redecorating gave us a pleasant feeling of approaching home. One of the first objects we saw, as we drew in to shore, was the long hull of the *Agamemnon*, and although in the stretches on opposite tacks—for the wind was easterly—she was often lost sight of, yet a day never passed without our seeing her now ahead, then astern, and it was clear the race would be a close one.

At Torbay a fishing-boat came alongside, and my husband proposed to land, and proceed by train to London. This course was referred to the captain, who advised us to remain till the ship reached the Isle of Wight, adding that, although easterly winds had set in, he would be able, with the tide, to work rapidly up the coast when he got a pilot on board.

On the 2nd June we were beating off the Isle of Wight, and stood in close to the shore. How barren the sea-board of other lands look when compared with that of England! Those who see for the first time such a country from the deck of a ship, must be charmed with the surprising cultivation presented by every promontory.

The land was intersected by lines cutting its surface into squares chequered like a chess-board, and the colours were the green of grass, the varying hue of growing grain, and the dark brown of the well-ploughed soil. The country rose and fell in graceful undulation—with clumps of trees, with white winding roads, with towns peeping from hollows, and villas nestling in foliage. After other realms it was a garden, not an ordinary storm-racked coast.

The captain, having resolved to anchor at Spithead for fresh meat and vegetables, steered for Portsmouth, after clearing the point. The last vessel whose signals the *Eastern Monarch* was destined to answer, was H. M. Screw Transport *Simoom*, that steamed past us for Gravesend. She had left Bombay with the invalids from that presidency, three weeks before we had left Kurrachee, and the captain was pleased to have beaten this ship by so long a period.

Next day we were to land, and our trunks were packed and ready to hand over the side. I retired to rest earlier than usual, anticipating fatigue and excitement. As I left the deck, the ship was moving gently through the water, on that calm summer's evening, with the distant and hazy outline of land around. About midnight I heard the cables as they ran out with that rumbling sound and tremulous motion by which we know that the heavy anchor of a large vessel is "let go," telling us that our voyage is accomplished, and we have safely reached England. Few, I imagine, can hear that sound without emotions of thankfulness for escape from past perils and for blessings received. But ours was not an ordinary return. How many had perished of every age and sex during the dreadful commotion through which we had been preserved! After a few solemn and grateful thoughts, I again fell asleep.

While my thoughts were roving back over dangers past, how little I suspected that the greatest peril I ever encountered was then kindled beneath me! My mind turned to battles, massacres, and cold-blooded murders. Did no shadow fall across it of explosion, and fire, and shipwreck? There were those lying asleep—young indeed—who must have been awakened when the ship's anchor was dropped on English soil—did any of these ideas pass through their minds, children though they were? Poor things, may their last waking sensations have been happy ones, for but a few minutes of time stood between them and eternity.

Never while I live, and my senses remain, can I forget my next awakening. Did I still dream, or was it indeed a reality? The whole ship seemed shattered into fragments—I was hurled from my bed, and I stood in the darkness of death. Is it the sea that bursts in a dense volume into the cabin? The decks seem to reel and quiver, to rise and fall. Now I thought it was perpendicular, then that the raging water was surging over its side up to the top. Stifled, I gasped for breath, the air was charged with sulphur, and the atmosphere such that it was death to remain. My mind became a moving panorama. The pictures are now indistinct, but, oh! how vividly my whole life passed on the shifting scenes, with one dreadful certainty, that it was death that was now dropping the curtain on my earthly stage. The most distinct feeling I remember of this moment of painful existence was—that this was death. Still, the whole period of the trance was but a moment; then instinct took the place of shattered reason, and it is amazing how rightly it guides.

I found my hand on the door; by a great effort I pushed it open, and a rush of fresh air cleared away from my brain much of the shock from which I was suffering. Immediately my husband was standing by my side, and amidst the stillness that followed I heard his voice as he called loudly to those on deck for the skylights to be raised. The cabin was in utter ruin, the tables shattered, the chairs broken, and the place strewed with fragments of glass. At my feet an awful chasm yawned. Far down I could see a bright glare that told the ship was on fire. The explosion had passed close by where we slept, torn up the decks, both this and that beneath, and blown away the after-companion ladder by which we gained the poop. Fragments of the brass balusters alone hung down, which my husband seizing, by a vigorous effort, he gained the poop; then, stooping down, he grasped my upraised hands, and in a few minutes I was lifted to the top. I felt as if the weight of worlds was in my limbs, and that I was powerless to struggle against the mountain crushing me down. My mind was keenly active, though my body was powerless, and I knew that it required the greatest exertion to raise me to the deck; yet I could do nothing to assist myself, though imagination kept vividly before me the picture of the awful fiery chasm down which I should be precipitated if my husband failed in his effort.

The change was sonething more than earthly when I stood on the deck, breathing the pure air, and looking on the tranquil shore of England, quietly resting, on this balmy morning, in the moon's soft light. I was there before the ship recovered from the shock; but then arose the wildest screams, and a tumult burst forth as if Bedlam had broken loose. I heard Colonel M. give directions to a soldier who rushed up, and I saw him grasp the arm of a man who staggered as if he would fall, and place him on a seat. This was the pilot, who had left the deck but an hour before for his first sleep for nights, when he was blown from the cuddy-table, where a bed had been made for him, through the skylight up to the poop. Then he disappeared, and I was left in the dress I had escaped in from my bed.

My mind was still full of a dreamy though vivid idea of the actual circumstances, but, by degrees, the full reality came before me. The ship was loaded with saltpetre. What! if another explosion should blow us into fragments! The dim coast was miles away, the fire rapidly gaining, and seven hundred human beings on board. "Can we all be saved?" I mentally exclaimed. "How dreadful the scene will be as it draws to its final close!" The ladies, escaping through the ports of their cabins, now began to reach the poop, and the ship was in indescribable commotion. To add to the alarm, a woman of unsound mind ran up the main gangway, uttering fearful cries. I turned towards her, and saw that in her arms she carried a child charred to a cinder. "It is not yours," exclaimed a soldier near. She immediately placed the little corpse on the deck, and speeded down again for her own little boy.

I looked on the water, and saw the tide rippling against the side as it flowed swiftly past. Away over the surface I could discern two or three small craft, and about half a mile off lay the black hull of a man-of-war steamer. My eyes were fixed on this vessel. With daylight I observed that the men on board were in rapid motion, and that boats were dropping into the water. Suddenly a light flashed over the sea, a flame burst from her port, followed by the loud roar of a heavy gun; then another and another, which rumbled in echoes along the slumbering shore, and awoke the inhabitants of Portsmouth. For the first time this sound came pleasantly on my ear, as that of the signal-guns of distress, not of the cannon of the enemy, and it spoke in tones of hope, as it broke on that coast always familiar with disasters and quick to rescue.

At first the only boat, except those the sailors had taken, was the cockle-shell of a pilot-schooner, which came alongside, and into which the ladies were directed to get. My husband had collected my clothes from the cabin, and pushed them through the companion-way, but he returned to obtain, if possible, some articles of value. The idea of the dangerous cargo, and the consequences that might follow at any moment, became fixed in my mind, and kept me in a state of intense anxiety.

The period he remained in the stifling smoke, now thickly penetrating into all the after-cabins, appeared hours to me, and as the things were packed up, I felt sure they could not be found. At last he emerged, dressed, with a tin uniform-box in his hand, containing many valuables. Eventually this was lost. It seemed sordid, while so many lives were in jeopardy, to devote time in the attempt to save such articles.

The dense throng of soldiers opened, and left a lane for the wives of their officers. As we were handed into the boat, and as I descended in a soldier's great-coat, and bare-footed, I saw the Colonel commanding the troops addressing the men and giving his orders. I well recollect the words that rang in my ears as we pushed off—"Remember, men, that you are British soldiers!"

When I stepped on the deck of the pilot-schooner, I was attired in the quaint costume I have described, but an addition was made to it by the kindness of one of the invalids, who lent me a pair of ammunition boots. The clothes Colonel M. had collected for me were lying on the deck of the ship. I had no time to put them on, and no inclination or power to carry them.

When I looked back, the ship was in a sheet of flame, her ports, as large as those of a frigate, being lit up with a dazzling glare. The fire had leaped along the rows of hammocks, from which the soldiers had sprung on the alarm, and a line of light shot along the water from each port, increasing as it went, till the whole blended into one, leaving all in brightness below, and all in darkness above, for a heavy cloud was gathering over the ship. Three thick volumes of smoke rose straight up from her graceful hull, and I could see over the bulwarks the dark forms of men hurrying to and fro in the black shade cast by the gathering cloud. Now and then a flame shot up amid pillars of smoke rising from the hatchways, disappeared as if choked, and then rose again higher than before.

Gradually, from the after-hatch, the flame became continuous; thé glare fell along the upper deck, and gave a red unearthly tinge to the strange shadows retreating before it. Sometimes it leaped aloft to the thick cloud drifting slowly with the wind; then the lurid light was thrown far over sea and land. Dense smoke arose from the hatchway near the forecastle, where now were grouped the whole throng of people. The little boats under the bowsprit looked like midges playing about the head of the great Indiaman. I could see figures springing wildly from the ship into the sea, where they were picked up by the boats, that seemed to fear too close a contact.

When I saw how little these boats could do, I watched with an eager anxiety—the anxiety that fixes the eye and clenches the hand—for I knew the time was short. The progress of the fire was appalling. The fitful flames rising from the hatches had become roaring volcanoes, and the ocean danced and glowed in a golden light. Higher and higher it sprang—caught the main-mast, and ran up aloft, playing gracefully in the rigging of the beautiful ship. The plentiful supply of varnish, French polish, and grease on the spars fed the fire, which darted up the mast, ran along the yards, and mingled with the dark cloud above. Then the mizen caught the flame—the ropes of the ship seemed to bear innumerable little balls of fire—and the rigging was illuminated as if for a holiday.

I turned from this absorbing spectacle, and strained my eyes in the direction of Portsmouth. For a minute I could see nothing but countless stars of light, and a feeling akin to despair took possession of my mind. Then the light broke gradually on my overstrained sight, and I could scarcely control my emotion on beholding a lugger under a press of sail bearing down in the morning breeze. My gaze was fixed on this vessel, and, with a beating heart, I watched her progress as she came gallantly on. Borne along both by the tide and the breeze, she ran swift and straight to the *Eastern Monarch*, and, turning rapidly under her jib-boom, the order rang out to "let go the anchor," which was dropped under the forecastle of the burning ship.

From every rope, from every projection, and down the sides of the tall Indiaman, came tumbling to the deck of the lugger the dense throng of soldiers, and in an incredibly short time, the forecastle was deserted, and all packed in the barge.

The flame sprang quickly on the fore-mast, and leaped up over the forecastle, as if hurrying to seize a prey it feared might escape; but its prey was gone. Already the bleat of the sheep and the scream of the pig were hushed in death; from stem to stern the conquering fire had enveloped the ship, and now nothing earthly could live on her raging hull.

A Brahman cow and a dear little gazelle were among the animals that perished. How gentle, pure, and high-bred both these sweet creatures were—the same colour, the same skin, and the same intelligent dark eyes in both. When I began to think of the loss of this night, the sad fate of these timid things came distressingly before me, though the noisy pigs might have claimed equal pity. Every effort was made by the lugger to get clear of the furnace, alongside which she was anchored, and I held my breath as the ship's mainmast swayed to one side, bowed itself forward, then took a greater bend to the side, and fell with a crash, bringing along with it the mizen, hissing into the boiling and bubbling water.

For a few minutes the solitary mast stood erect, wrapt in flame, then swayed like its fellows, and like them fell hissing into the sea. With the towering spars went the beauty of the scene—the noble vessel was a dismal wreck! But the fire that had consumed the deck now sprang up from the cargo with still greater violence, and the heat was felt hundreds of yards around. Far off, in the Isle of Wight, and in Hampshire, the people were startled at the illumination over the great arsenal of the British navy; and many rose to see if it was the light of the morning that burst with so strong a glare into their rooms.

I could scarcely credit the fact that all this was the work of one short hour. These few minutes only were required for the destruction of the finest and strongest of England's merchant ships, and for the disembarkation of the seven hundred souls who but an hour before had been quietly sleeping in what now seemed a volcano raging on the sea. The ladies removed to the *Falcon*, and I had there the pleasure of meeting my husband, and of hearing that all had been saved except seven, killed by the explosion, and many hurt by the unavoidable accidents inevitable on such occasions.

An officer of rank arrived in a small steamer, with orders for the *Falcon* to sink the *Eastern*

Monarch. The man-of-war, whose steam was up, ranging alongside, drove her shot between the wind and water, but the blazing ship lightened as she burnt, and the shot holes in the water line gradually rose. They were afraid the fiery furnace they failed to sink might break from her cables and drift among the shipping.

We were transferred to a small steamer, which ran into the basin, and I landed at Portsmouth, in the borrowed military cloak and ammunition boots, neither of them mine. I had literally no clothes of my own as I again set foot in my native country.

Those who ally themselves to the career of a soldier must be prepared for quick and startling changes. After such an unexpected calamity I felt truly thankful for my happy and safe arrival. What a contrast had been effected in a few short hours! Another great peril had been added to those which had so lately encompassed me—another peril encountered and past—another mercy vouchsafed, and one that deepened my gratitude to the Protecting Hand that had been stretched out in my defence, and in that of another life I held so dear.

As I looked out to sea, a huge tower of vapour

shot into the heavens from the burning ship. The long-dreaded explosion had come at last; the dangerous cargo had ignited, and burst with a force that would have blown the decks into fragments, had decks still been there. For two days the ship remained on fire, then it gradually died out, leaving nothing of the noble vessel, which had been towed to the shore, save a blackened shell stranded on the beach. The last I saw of the ship so long my home was in that tall sulphurous column which had risen from the mine over which I had calmly slept for many months.

But though in reality I never again saw the ill-fated *Eastern Monarch*, this scene often came back in my dreams. I again trembled at the dreadful explosion, again listened to the piercing screams, again beheld the busy throng struggling for life, and again witnessed the stern discipline of the army, the authority of the officers even in this extremity prevailing. One fearful nightmare settled on my sleep, though it was weeks before I knew the full extent of the shock I had sustained. The nerves, so long strained, seemed unable to bear this pressure, and were, I feared, injured for ever. My hair fell off in handfuls. In that hour years were added to my life, and nothing but a mother's supporting kindness could have soothed the desponding state into which I sank.

The people of Portsmouth, deeply interested in the losses of the returned Indian soldiers, came kindly forward to their relief, and several ladies called to offer us their houses and their clothes.

But I was eager to get home, and I hurried up to London that evening, where we found some difficulty in obtaining a bed. It was Epsom race week, the hotels were full, and the metropolis thronged. The waiters looked suspiciously at our attire, and I fear their suspicion was confirmed when they saw there was not an article of baggage on the cab. There was something dreary and disheartening beyond expression in such a return to our own land. It seemed as if the misfortune which entitled us to the hand of kindness caused us to be shunned where we had most expected to meet with a hearty reception. After driving to many hotels, where we were assured we could not obtain accommodation, we left it to the cabman, who took us to a house in Cork Street, where the good Samaritans gave us the rooms we required.

I retired to rest, but found it not. Not for one moment did I sleep. Though my frame was sinking with fatigue, my imagination was working in a way I had never before known, and I could scarcely refrain from crying aloud when some dreadful picture of the conflagration passed through my mind.

All that night I heard the ceaseless roll of carriages in the distance, as the great stream ebbed and flowed along Piccadilly, broken now and then by a louder rattle when a cab went over the pavement of our street.

I rose early in the morning, and when the shops opened, obtained the necessaries I required, got our letters from the agents, and fast as the Great Western could carry me, hastened to my home.

CHAPTER XI.

Embarkation at Liverpool for Canada—The *Anglo-Saxon* and her Passengers—Fogs off Newfoundland—Icebergs—Quebec and its Scenery—Disappointment—Falls of Montmorenci—Citadel of Quebec and its Garrison—Steaming to Montreal—Yankee Barber—Kingstown—Arrival at Toronto—Opening of the University—State of the Country—Niagara Falls Station—Blondin and the Great Cataract—Primeval Forest.

SHORTLY after our arrival, I had to decide whether I would accompany my husband to Canada, on a visit to his father, or remain in England. At first I shrank from the sea, but I found with surprise that the impression left by the wreck of the *Eastern Monarch*, gradually, after a period of great depression, softened into the remembrance of a startling adventure I had a hazy idea had happened to myself. Much to the astonishment of my friends, I decided on going. In fact, half the period I propose to relate was spent on the ocean. My voyages seemed interminable, only ending to recommence. As shipwreck is a probable occurrence to the sailor, so it became to me. Does not such a life make gipsies of us all, creating an unsettled feeling that pines for the excitement of travel?

On the 26th July, 1859, we embarked at Liverpool in the *Anglo-Saxon*, one of the Montreal line; and on receiving the mail, steamed round the north of Ireland, quickly getting into the long swell of the boisterous Atlantic.

Compared with the Indian voyage, this trip is a trifle, and the arrangements made by the passengers are in accordance. There was scarcely a point of resemblance between the noble sailing ship so lately my home, and the mail steamer. Instead of the large cabin of the *Eastern Monarch*, with its carpet, sofa, and plate-glass port, through which I looked over the ocean as from a drawing-room window, I was now in what they called a state room, with berths rising in tiers one over the other, ventilated by a shaft from the deck, lighted by frosted glass fixed in the door opening on the passage, and at night by a triangular lamp made to do the triple duty of illuminating my cabin, the next one, and the passage. The care of this lamp was entrusted to invisible hands, who lighted and extinguished it when it pleased themselves.

On deck the towering masts and wide spread of canvas of the Indiaman were in striking contrast with the low masts and little sail of the large ocean packet. The sea itself was different. Every arrangement of the one vessel was made for storm and cold, of the other for fine weather and heat. The steamer was built for carrying a large number with speed on a short voyage, the East Indiaman for carrying few with comfort on a long one.

Nor was this the only change, as I found when I joined my fellow-passengers. For years I had been accustomed to a society where officers of the Army greatly preponderated, thus giving to it a peculiar and professional tone. They were the only passengers in the *Eastern Monarch* except the two or three ladies, their wives. On meeting in the *Anglo-Saxon*, it was clear that the colonial element prevailed, and that the feeling, thoughts, and conversation of the passengers were cast in another mould.

When I came on board I found a rush being

made into the saloon, and the reason disclosed itself at dinner, the first in the race being nearest to the captain, and I, who now discovered that "knowledge is power," certainly in the matter of seats, was far away at the end. Further experience taught me that the gain was not worth the trouble of hustling in this unseemly haste, for in these cheap and well-found ships the attendance is good and the food ample. This formed another point of difference between the *Eastern Monarch* and the *Anglo-Saxon*, the passage-money in the Indiaman being exorbitantly high, and the table not to be compared with that of the steamers of this cheap line.

In a week we were passing to the north of Newfoundland, and, as usual, in a heavy fog. The shrill whistle connected with the engine rang out its harsh and grating scream as the ship rushed over the water. I asked one of the officers if there were any icebergs near.

"Not many at this season," he replied; "I hardly think we shall see any."

The fog lifted, the sun came dull and hazy through, then darkened, and at last came gradually out. The mist seemed to rise off the ocean, the blue sky peeped brightly forth, a ripple curled the sea, and in a short time nothing of the fog remained but a heavy bank to leeward. Shining like little white islands in the sun, the sea was dotted with icebergs. We passed close by some, whose great fields of spotless snow dazzled the spectator. Others reared icy pinnacles, glittering aloft, and showed dark caves in their perpendicular sides, as they drifted slowly by.

Before night the ship was again enveloped in fog, and I had little pleasure in the vicinity of such dangerous neighbours, and little confidence in the shrill scream announcing our approach. Whatever heed the fisherman might give to the intimation that a steamer was running down on him, it was clear that the icebergs would turn a deaf ear to the signal. Early next morning I heard a commotion on deck. The fog had lifted, and straight on our course lay one of those floating islands, whose projecting sides almost grazed us as we went by.

On the 3rd August we made Belleisle, and for four days steamed up the estuary of the St. Lawrence, sighting the desolate coast of Labrador, and the dreary island of Anticotti. It was midnight when we moored to the bank close to the terminus of the Grand Trunk Railway, separated from Quebec by the flood of the great river.

It is not my intention to sketch scenery that has formed a subject for many able pens. I rapidly turn over the leaves of my journal, and pause but to make a few selections.

Quebec has more the appearance of an old and dirty European town than of the mushroom growth of the American continent. There is a great contrast between its worn and antiquated look, and the new-fangled Yankee notions with which it seems to be impregnated. Here was the old fort, looking down on the precipitous old streets. There I heard the *patois* French, and saw the quaint old vehicles on the stand, that must have been invented before the time of the revolution. Yet there was a Yankee air, ideas, and manners, I could not fail to observe. The hotel where we put up was in the usual American style—a large ill-furnished room, with guide-books scattered about, puffing watering-places and hotels, a piano, with a young lady playing, a *table d'hôte*, and a bar, with its loungers, tobacco, slings, and cobblers.

On the whole, I was disappointed with the

scenery. The dreary vastness of Labrador was only toned down in the richer and more cultivated vastness here. It may be prejudice, nursed by our limited island home, that makes me shrink from interminable wastes. The land on the St. Lawrence, to me, was poor and wild enough, but my imagination carried me back into the solitudes, far away, of perpetual winter—solitudes of which the sterile wilderness of Labrador was the type. With a cold shudder I recalled how immense was the domain, too wild even for the savage, and how limited the circle of civilization. As the incongruous mixture of the old with the new grated on me in the town, so the comparison of the grandeur of nature with the paltry works of man grated on me in the country. In a new settlement, in rapid progress, the mind takes hold of the future, and in the rough and crude beginnings sees the infancy of a nation. Here, with the rawness of a new country, there was an air of age that told of progress arrested, and seemed to refuse either a history past, or a history to come.

First impressions may be strongly influenced by disappointed expectations. To me Quebec was an over-praised place. I had seen its scenery described in rapturous terms, and heard it spoken of as the most pleasant quarter in an empire that embraced the globe. I had been led to expect too much, and I was disappointed.

Coming up from the estuary, the river narrows till both banks can be seen—to the right, barren and hilly; to the left, low and wooded, with long lines of white close to the water, shewing the villages, bnt with little cultivation, of which there was none on the opposite site.

A rock close to an island in the channel had been fatal to one of these Montreal steamers .The wreck lay with the bow high up, and the stern immersed in the water. The number of vessels lost by the Company proves the dangerous nature of the navigation, but it is to be hoped nothing may check the progress of this most useful line.

We drove to the Falls of Montmorenci. The stream rushes down a rocky hill, and precipitates itself over the scarp cut away by the St. Lawrence, falling in a feathery white plume into the channel a few miles below Quebec. It is a charming scene, and worthy of the renown it has acquired. In winter, the drifting shower from the streaming foam falls in snow flakes clear of the water, and piles up a hill of frost. Over the frozen St. Lawrence the citizens delight to direct their sleighs, and officers and their "muffins" feel the greatest pleasure in each other's society.

The citadel of Quebec crowns the apex formed by the St. Lawrence and a small tributary. The plateau is a few hundred feet above the level of the great river, and falls precipitously to its bed. The town stands at the junction below the Fort, and creeps up the hill to its very walls. I had exaggerated the scene of Wolfe's exploit. To my mind's eye the height had been greater, the ascent more steep. On the top Abram's Plain gave a fair field to the opposing forces. A simple monument has been erected on the spot stained with the life-blood of the English general, with the simple inscription—"Here died Wolfe victorious."

The residence of the Governor-General is situated about three miles from the town, where the plain slopes gradually to the water. Spencer Wood appeared to me a poor edifice for so exalted an official, although the beauty of the spot redeems the poverty of the building.

A wing of the Canadian Rifles occupied the

citadel, and my husband took the opportunity of paying a visit to a regiment his father had commanded a short time before. From the Fort we looked down on the mighty river, and over an extent of country that added grandeur to the beauty of the picture it presented. I was surprised at the prodigious quantity of timber; wherever I went, I passed acres of logs; they were moored in huge rafts along the shore, or stranded in fields on the mud of the tributary. Ships, too, in all stages of growth, were rising from these logs under the axe and hammer of the workmen. When finished, they are loaded with logs similar to those from which they have been created, and the whole mass, raw and manufactured, seeks its market in England.

We had taken our passage at Liverpool by the St. Lawrence steamers to Toronto, and we embarked and proceeded to Montreal. These boats had been so accurately described that I knew them. The lower deck, with its engine-room; the offices, and the ladies' cabin; the upper deck, with its dining saloon, state rooms, and open space to the bow and stern; the hurricane deck, with its box for the man at the wheel placed close to the bow;

the iron see-saw and the paddle-boxes appeared familiar, although experience had taught me the difficulty of forming a correct idea of a thing not seen before. When the great see-saw began to rise and fall, like the arms of a giant, the huge paddles spun through the water, and we shot with railway speed up the stream, the light structure throbbing under the powerful propulsion.

The land was hedged off in long narrow strips running back from the river, as if a little frontage and a great depth had been allotted to each occupant. The double towers of a Roman Catholic Church stood on a very commanding spot, with its tin-covered roof glittering strangely in the sun. This was the only large building among the numerous white and pretty villages, cottages, and farm-houses we passed.

All my admiration, which grew with my knowledge of the colony, was centred in one object. Unlike the muddy Ganges, or wide-spread and meandering Indus, the noble St. Lawrence rolls down a flood equal to them both, between strong and rocky banks, pure and clear as a crystal stream. In any Eastern land the St. Lawrence would be worshipped as a god. No other river in America, nor, indeed, in the world, can be compared with it —not for its banks, but for its waters. Here it spreads out into a bright blue lake, across which it is impossible to see; there the steamer winds amid numerous islets, then rushes down rapids—roaring, boiling, and foaming—mighty almost as the ocean. Again it spreads out deep, broad, and calm, sufficient to bear to the sea the commerce of a continent. The day must come when this river will be associated with the poetry of a nation —perhaps of many nations. That poetry must be of a high order to be worthy of the subject.

Montreal is the finest city of Canada, and, although inferior to Melbourne or Sydney, stands next, I imagine, in the order of our colonial towns. The *Anglo-Saxon* was blowing off her steam as we moored, a vessel of the largest class lying at a wharf hundreds of miles up the stream. Of course the structure that first attracts the eye is the tubular bridge which connects the Grand Trunk Railway from Portland to Lake Huron. It is seen in its entire length of a mile and a half, and has a light graceful appearance, although one of the most stupendous works ever put together. The piers have to withstand the flood of the St. Lawrence, bearing against them vast blocks of ice, the artillery of the river, at the same time that they support the heavy traffic.

While our steamer was getting through the numerous locks of the Lachine Canal we wandered over the town.

The first shop we entered in America was a hairdresser's, to have our hair washed after the voyage. One of the shopmen said,

"I guess you have newly arrived?"

When I assented, he pointed to another.

"That gentleman comes from London—where, I calculate, he's pretty generally known."

On looking over the lists of arrivals at the hotels, I noticed that the Smiths and Browns of the States entered the grand and simple word "New York" after their names. In Europe American ideas take a wider range, and Dr. Jones styles himself a citizen of the United States, and "calculates that if he's wanted he will be found there." Already they have brought into fashion the habit of applying the word *American* to signify a native of the United States. Considering that the continent extends from Terra del Fuego to the North Pole, it would not be more arrogant in the French to usurp for themselves exclusively the term *European*, regarding all the rest of that continent as outsiders.

We proceeded, by the cars, to Lachine. Names that at first grated on my ear became, ere long, the correct words, and "cars" eventually sounded more appropriate than "trains" and "railway-carriages." The novel shape, the single line of rails, scarcely protected by a fence from the intrusion of animals, the peculiar chimney of the engine, with its broad-mouthed funnel, and the strange structure in front called a cow-catcher, arrested my attention.

The canal work was slow and tiresome; but when the steamer was fairly in the river, she made the most surprising way.

Shortly after leaving Ontario the river bursts through a country that appears to have vigorously resisted its passage through it, and still keeps up its opposition, in little rocky and wooded islets, which may be counted by the hundred. The water frets and boils against these barriers, winding and twisting through them in numberless channels. The Thousand Islands form a scene of great beauty, yet it has been over-painted.

We touched at Kingston, where the river widens

as if about to enter the sea, instead of leaving a lake, and we walked ashore into the town. The streets were lonely and deserted, giving rather an impression of decay than of the bustle and progress of a colonial town.

Besides the finest river in the world Canada has the finest lakes; and pretty and rich as some parts of the province are, there is more to be admired in its waters than in its land. All night we were crossing Lake Ontario at the rate of seventeen miles an hour. Blue as the ocean, and as unfathomed, without an object on the horizon to break the meeting of sky and water around, stretched out the magnificent lake, and for hours and hours the steamer passed over its surface with the speed of a bird.

Day was breaking when the lighthouse of Toronto rose in sight, and we were close to the city when I came on deck. Yet I could not discern a vestige of the place, save a few specks on the horizon, which grew into trees, then came out as a line of land, gradually assuming the aspect of a city, almost on a level with the water, with rising ground behind. A long belt of sand suddenly appeared between us and the capital of Western Canada. The steamer steered straight on the line, and went at full speed through a passage that had sunk from the spit, which I saw enclosed a fine sheet of water, the harbour of Toronto. Through the clear lake the submerged portion, that has so unaccountably sunk, was visible. Some dread is entertained that this natural sea-wall against the stormy waters of the lake may be swept away by the action of the waves. Toronto lay stretched along the shore with an imposing appearance from the water. It is marked out in long straight streets, running parallel with the lake, and crossed, at right angles, by others of less importance—all broad, and planted with young trees. They are Macadamized, but, as the metal does not bind well, they are covered with loose stones. For the first time I saw miles of boards laid down as footpaths, two or three of the best streets only being flagged. The great thoroughfare is King Street, which would be considered a fine street in any capital. Those accustomed to the high finish of everything in England are often disappointed, but unreasonably so, in seeing little of it in the colonies, where a landscape is seldom perfect or a street finished. On one side, King Street is composed of good and even noble buildings; on the other, it is poor and incomplete. Opposite the gigantic hotel, the Bossin House, are a few wooden sheds, and an open space where rubbish is cast. The shops are very good, showing a display of meat, fish, game, vegetables, and fruit, cheaper in price and better in quality than similar provisions in any other colony. I think it is in the abundant supply of the best provisions that Canada excels. The high duties paid on English goods make articles of clothing dear, but the shops of drapers and others are conducted on the English system, and I saw few of those detestable establishments called stores.

I was at the opening of the University—a building of which the Canadians may well be proud. It stands in what will be a handsome park, connected with the city by a broad avenue thickly lined with trees. Those who have seen Cape Town can form an opinion of the advantage and ornament to a city which such avenues afford. I hope this habit of decorating the streets with trees will be maintained here, and imitated in other climates where the sun strikes with as hot a glare.

The public buildings are numerous and handsome. Among them, throughout the colony, I was struck with the size of the lunatic asylums. On observing their spacious dimensions, it might be supposed that the rulers of the land expected a large proportion of the population to go mad, and had prepared for their future accommodation. Schools, colleges, churches, and lunatic asylums are everywhere fine; government-houses, barracks, forts, are poor, as far as I saw, not even excepting the Citadel of Quebec. Some beautiful private houses were rising in the neighbourhood; a few of a very high order of domestic architecture. I think the people in Western Canada live in excellent houses.

Toronto is a good type of the colony; too large, wanting in concentration, in short, most unprofitably spread out. The owner of land near the centre holds for an extravagant price; the owner at a distance entices buyers by every inducement. Thus large spaces in the town are unoccupied, and houses cover the blocks where cattle should graze; gas-lamps flare over corn-fields; and wooden pathways border the meadow of the dairy cow. The inhabitants may well complain of the town-rates.

No pleasant roads wind through the country in

the vicinity. One or two long streets take a course nearly parallel with the lake, and one or two more run in the other direction towards the back country. In England they would be called roads; why in Canada are they termed streets? To me the pecularity of the town was the want of cultivation in the neighbourhood, the land around being chiefly in a state of nature. Scarcely a field is to be seen, and over the wide areas which ought to be filled with neat country houses and villas, with their ornamental grounds, stand sign-boards informing the passersby that they are eligible investments, soon to become the centre of the city. The growth of potatoes and turnips does not interfere with the sale of these eligible investments —why, then, should not farming operations go on even in regions destined to so grand a future?

The land speculating fever has had something to do with a state of things so damaging to the appearance and even to the interests of the city. A collapse had just followed the late balloon-like ascent of the colony, and many of the speculators found themselves in the air. Extensive towns on paper had grown iñ every direction around, and the wanderer in the environs often tripped over the pegs that marked streets with high-sounding names. The lots went from tens of pounds to hundreds, then began to assume the importance of "feet frontage," and finally reverted to their agricultural merits, leaving the owners in blank dismay, regarding their paper towns as the possessor of a bank-note, when payment was stopped, might regard the highly artistic and illuminated paper promising to pay.

The sand wall to which Toronto owes so much runs from the swampy land at the east end parallel with the beach, and therefore facing the city built along the shore of the excellent harbour it forms. All the land around Ontario is low—that in this neighbourhood is very low. Some three miles from the shore the country rises suddenly about one hundred feet. On the crest of the plateau many large country houses are situated. The soil, particularly to the east, is of a light sandy nature, ill adapted for roads. An extensive and well-laid out cemetery lies in this direction. The contemptible fort stands at the west end, where the barracks also are. It is intended to throw its shot across the entrance of the harbour, but this intention has been defeated by the chasm formed by Nature in the sand spit.

There are two routes to Niagara—that by the Lake, and that by the Great Western Railway. As the weather was oppressively hot, we chose the cool waters of Ontario, and were carried by the *Zimmerman* to Lewiston, at the entrance of the river. My first journey on this lake had been made at night; now I crossed in the day, and could scarcely realize the fact that I was borne over fresh water, as the vessel rolled, pitched, and throbbed in the swell; while the meeting of the water and the sky was unbroken by a single object. The blue was not so deep as that of the ocean—more that of ultramarine. Again the little black specks rose on the horizon, and quickly formed themselves into a low line of coast. We entered the river, and passed the United States fort, stopping at the place where the cars that left on the arrival of the steamer stood ready to receive us.

It was night when we reached the Niagara Falls Station. Rooms had been already engaged for us at the Clifton House, as this hotel was filled with Americans, and chance arrivals could not always be accommodated. Wherever we went we found numbers of Yankee tourists passing over the country. They had settled in crowds at Niagara. It is the custom of this lively and energetic people to get into motion after midsummer, and stream away from home in all directions. I was told that the young and pretty women accompany the men in these tours, and that the old and ugly remain at home. These flittings have become a necessity that must be gratified at any cost; and among the poorer classes every dollar is scraped together for the summer migration. These yearly pleasure trips are one of the excellent results of quick and cheap locomotion. It is no wonder that guide-books use high-flown language to puff the routes it is their interest to recommend, and that hotels employ every means to intercept and delay the streams of passengers.

I cannot describe with what interest I waited for the rising of the moon, that I might see the Falls by its light. The verandah of my bedroom faced the cataract, and its roar was in my ear, and even its white gleam before my eyes, but I could make out nothing distinctly. The sound of the falling flood filled the air, and was so continuous that I grew to think it natural, and would have been surprised and alarmed had it ceased. It was a sort of lullaby in my sleep all night, though I awoke with a start as its deep soft melody came on me at once.

I got up, and prepared myself for the overwhelming sight, then walked into the verandah, and stood before the Falls of Niagara.

Is there any sight that can bear such a preparation, except those that awake a sense of fear? I confess to a feeling of disappointment; but the grand as well as the beautiful, in Nature as in art, grows on the beholder; so the longer I remained, the more deeply I became impressed, and I even feel that I left Niagara with an estimate far below that of its real magnificence. I consider that ordinary minds require time to form a just appreciation of the sublime scene.

After breakfast I walked up the bank, and saw the rapids as the mighty river came leaping over rocks and stones in a broad impetuous rush, growing awful as it neared the chasm. Above the fall the banks rise very little. Below, they stand on each side like steep walls, equal in height to the Fall, from which I conclude that it has been formed by the water cutting away the lower level till it has assumed its present aspect, not by the stream precipitating itself from a higher into a lower range of country.

When Blondin walked across the fall on a rope, it was below, not over or above the cataract, where a rope could not be fixed. The great acrobat had announced publicly that he would walk on a rope stretched across this chasm, with a man on his back. Tens of thousands assembled to witness the feat. People were inclined to think it a hoax, yet Toronto, Hamilton, and London poured out their inhabitants on the Canadian bank, while the citizens of Buffalo, Rochester, and other large towns, assembled on the American shore.

The rope was stayed by guys that made it look like the web of a spider, so thin and gossamer appeared Blondin's pathway over the gigantic gap, more than a thousand feet wide. It required an opera-glass to distinguish him as he stood on the American side, with a balancing pole in his hand. He advanced, springing into the air, and throwing somersaults, till he gained the space beyond the network of guys, to either bank, that steadied the rope. Then he appeared as if standing in air, midway in the dark cleft. Suddenly his position was reversed; and he was seen hanging by his heels, with his head to the raging flood.

I looked down to the black water, and there was the *Maid of the Mist*, like a bubble on its surface, swaying to and fro, though steaming little short of full power. The crowd of white, upturned faces on her deck must have seen the acrobat as a speck in the sky. He crossed to our side, and, after a brief rest, placed straps on his shoulders, supporting a seat, on which his companion mounted. The face of the latter was pale, as they proceeded to execute their perilous exploit. The sensation was almost sickening as Blondin cautiously moved down the incline, for, however tight, no stretching could make the rope straight.

The interest was painful, and increased when he found a difficulty in disengaging the balancing pole from the guys. Afterwards he stopped, and, amidst breathless suspense, the rider dismounted and stood on the rope, allowing Blondin to rest. The man mounted and dismounted several times before the task was completed.

For months after the American newspapers recorded accidents to citizens ambitious of rivaling this feat. Rope-walking became the fashion, and some absurd attempts were made by tyros in imitation of Blondin. But the most characteristic circumstance connected with this performance was a hoax put forth by a Buffalo paper, in which the public were laughed at for believing the story, said to be merely concocted for their amusement. This was circulated as a fact throughout the country, and even in England, where I was surprised to hear people observe, "I thought that story was untrue."

The Clifton House is a good hotel, though I dislike the American system, which cannot be other than disagreeable to English tastes. When an Englishman arrives in America he soon finds how little liberty he is to enjoy. Freedom is for the crowd, slavery for the individual. The ductile and pliable nature swims with the stream; he of strong opinions and set habits struggles against it, but his liberty is what the torrent gives—he must get out of it or drown. My chief objections to American hotels are the want of privacy, and the want of independent action. The only room where I could escape the crowd was my bedroom, which was without furniture, and the idea of a waiter answering a bell was so absurd as to call forth a smile of derision. The men crowded the billiard-room and bar, and every new acquaintance asked Colonel M. what he would take. The theory seemed to be that he had a never-failing thirst for cock-tails and juleps.

When we were leaving we asked for an early dinner, and were told it could not be served. Let any one come in late, and see what fare he will get. The custom of forcing all into one channel may answer admirably for the hotel-keeper, but it is one that the instinct of the English rebels against. The Clifton House could no more have accommodated the same number of English people in English style, than a village inn could accommodate the visitors to the Grosvenor Hotel.

The heat was so intense that the people were confined to the house during mid-day. The ladies amused themselves by dressing. After exhibiting in the extreme of the Parisian mode I supposed they were dressed for the day. It required a good look at the individual to be certain she was the same whose gaudy plumage had been changed since the morning. Why should travellers dress in this way, who come to see one of the grandest sights of nature, situated in a wild and thinly peopled country?

As we were returning to Lewiston, a man entered the car, and, in the voice of a showman, directed us to look to the right, and we should see the column on the hill-side where the Yankees had been defeated by the forces of the British and the Canadian volunteers. I thought this in bad taste, but, on inquiry, I learned it was a habit in the States for the conductors to point out the fields claimed by the Americans, often in the most extravagant language, and sometimes with as much truth as the Yankees might claim Bull's Run.

The road took us through the primeval forest, and between vast fields of Indian corn, enclosed in snake-fences, presenting to me a novel, and, in many places, a most beautiful landscape. I was alarmed by the car stopping. My mind being filled with collisions, and with anxiety, I tried to discover the cause. A man ran down the line, and was asked the reason of the stoppage.

"I lost a straw hat hereabouts yesterday, and I want to see if I can find it!"

I was surprised; however, one soon gets over these surprises in America.

The village of Lewiston had the same deserted appearance, on a small scale, that Kingston had on a large. When there we looked for the *Zimmerman*. The vessel was advertised to start punctually on the arrival of the train, due at 7 P.M. She was not to be seen, however, having taken a party of pleasure for an excursion on the lake.

"I calculate," added our informant, "that she will be back by ten o'clock to-night."

Wearied and hungry we went to the inn for tea. The meal was in keeping with the poverty-stricken look of the place—it was a vinegar tea. There was beet-root in vinegar, cucumber in vinegar, and other vegetables, all steeped in this acid. Whatever I tasted was sour, and I rose from the table feeling vinegary myself.

The steamer returned about half-past ten, and had to replenish the fuel exhausted. It was about midnight, therefore, when this passenger-boat, advertised to sail at 7 P.M., started, and no one thought of complaining—for this is American liberty!

CHAPTER XII.

Grand Trunk Railway—Impressions of Canada—Return to England—The English Eleven, and the Yankee Twenty-two—Chinese Expedition—On board the *White Star*—Off Ireland—The Surgeon-Major and his School—Eclipse of the Sun—Good Ships in a Storm—Moon Blindness—Visit to Anjer—Dutch Formality—Pulo Sapeta.

One of the pleasant points of Canada is the certainty of constant and speedy intelligence, every second or third day bringing a mail from Europe. We were startled by the news of our defeat at the Peiho, and visions arose of another campaign in China. As Colonel M. knew the war was certain, and the employment of a battalion of the Sixtieth probable, he became eager to return, that he might be able to join at the earliest notice.

The Indian summer had passed by, and the cold of the Canadian winter was commencing. The autumn tints of the trees were lovely beyond description. The leaves do not simply wither, or lose their brilliant green, but they turn to a different hue, equally brilliant—some yellow, some scarlet, some brown—till the whole forest flames like a gallery of Turner's paintings.

Having come up by the river, we decided on returning to Quebec by the railway. On the 28th October we left Toronto by seven A.M. train, arriving at Quebec in twenty-four hours. I dare say the Grand Trunk Railway is the most ambitious work ever executed in a new country. I know nothing of the history of the undertaking, but I regarded it as the effort of a number of patriots to bestow upon the land a benefit that would be felt for generations. Ignorant of the resources of the country, I was doubtful whether so widely-scattered a community could afford to keep the rail in working order. From Toronto to Quebec, the best part of the year, there is the finest water communication in the world. The rail, nearly in its whole course, runs through the virgin forest, and no doubt gives value to land that will, some day, be brought into profitable cultivation; but a country must be very populous that can afford to construct long lines of rail where there is good water carriage.

In consequence of the facilities furnished by the great rivers, travelling is cheaper in America than in any other country. Even in the populous states, can a railway pay a large dividend to its shareholders that has to compete directly with one of those rivers?

The impression left on my mind by Canada was that of a large flat country, with good land and a pleasant climate; both of which gradually deteriorate as the sea is neared, till they change into the wintry and sterile region of Labrador, or the poor and cold province of Nova Scotia. The waters of Ontario, Erie, and Huron surround the best portion, which is connected with the sea by the St. Lawrence and the Grand Trunk Railway. Its climate is modified from the extremes of the States, by the vast expanse of water, and it stretches into the best latitudes. It is either level or slightly undulating, but generally in a waste state. It is all, or nearly all, covered with timber. Without doubt it is one of the fairest regions of North America, yet the main stream of emigration has flowed in another direction, viz., to the prairies of the States. The reason is simple, The Canadian lands are covered with a dense forest—the prairie lands are open, and ready for the plough. The Canadian settler, hewing his farm from the bush, sees, in his cleared two hundred acres, the labour of a life, such as none, except those reared to toil, can accomplish. The prairie settler commences at the point which the Canadian attains to only after the labour of years.

There is much that is beautiful in many of the counties, with their undulating ground here and there cleared, here and there covered with timber; scenes that present a very different aspect to the dreary wastes of the prairie states. Small streams are scarce, though I have seen many picturesque villages planted by flowing water, with their grist and saw mills, their rough snake fences, their corn-fields and fine cattle, combining to give a pleasing impression of an agricultural land; and I have nowhere seen a more teeming abundance than in this favoured province.

The weather was cold at Toronto when we started, and it was winter when we arrived next day at Quebec. All was frost, and the change was so great that it was difficult to recognize the country in which we had landed so short a period before. We had taken our passage in the *North Briton*, the last packet to leave the St. Lawrence, for the season had arrived when that river ceased to be a highway. The ship was lying in the stream, deeply laden with peas—so deeply that I looked at her with dread when I thought of the stormy passage before me. In my journal, day after day, I find these words repeated, "Heavy gale." Indeed, the season was more than usually stormy, and attended with wrecks that threw the nation into mourning. Among others, perished that ill-fated ship the *Royal Charter*, and the spot where so many lives were lost, but a few days before, was pointed out by the pilot. The vessel of this line, that crossed us in her outward passage, went on her way to a disastrous shipwreck; and the days of that in which we sailed were numbered, for she met the end that had overtaken so many of her sister steamers in the great estuary of the St. Lawrence.

We arrived at Liverpool on the 11th of November, and the neatness and finish of everything struck us with a charming freshness. The roads, hedges, fields, houses, looked like garden-work after the roughness of Canada. The Americans are right in the tone they assume when they talk of the great natural features of their country, and sink their pretensions to the civilization of Europe. The grandeur of their rivers, lakes, and forests impress an Englishman, who turns with a sneer from the towns and the farms they so extravagantly praise.

A young lady was in the steamer that took us out, who spoke with enthusiasm of her own dear Canada, the land of her birth, and where she had lived till within the last two years. At Toronto, where I had the pleasure of renewing the acquaintance, I found her raptures had toned down. She had not exaggerated the grandeur of the lake over which she looked from her bed-room windows, nor the beauty of the forest in its autumn tints, but her eye had become accustomed to the refinement of England, and, on her return, she saw the rudeness of which she had before been unconscious.

Among the passengers we landed were the "All England Eleven," who had been challenged by twenty-two cricketers of the States. The match had excited much interest in Canada. The Americans were surprised and mortified when they found what mere children they were at the game in the skilled hands of their adversaries. That twenty-two Americans could be defeated in anything by eleven English, was quite incomprehensible to them; and their newspapers found only one way to account for the fact. They inquired into the birth of the twenty-two, and then boldly asserted that there was not a native American among them! If this be true, it fully proves that there is no such thing as a Yankee cricketer.

The result was telegraphed to Toronto, and furnished an "extra" for the newspapers. There I heard little boys crying,

"The Yankee twenty-two skinned alive by the English eleven!"

Verily there is no love lost between British America and the United States.

The China expedition was fitted out in India, and the details were settled in that country. Some time elapsed before we ascertained that the 2nd Battalion was to form a part. When it was known, an application from Colonel M. to join at once met with prompt attention at the Horse-

Guards, and he was booked for the April steamer. Unfortunately for him, there were no means of getting away at once, and what he dreaded came to pass.

If the campaign were protracted, or a prolonged occupation followed the capture of Peking, the regiments employed would require re-inforcements. It would be necessary to send officers with the soldiers—therefore, till he could get away, there was a chance of his being detained for this duty.

He was not left long in suspense. Orders were issued for detachments to prepare for embarkation; the passage for my husband was countermanded, and he was directed to proceed with the recruits for Hong-Kong. This was a bitter disappointment, for he felt confident he could not be in time for the campaign. He knew that, without the honour and advantage of the Field Service, most of its disagreeables would fall to the lot of those who were to hold the conquests till terms could be enforced. The only course was to bear patiently the change, and try to extract from it whatever advantages it offered.

I had anticipated the separation with dismay; I now saw with pleasure a hope of accompanying my husband. The ship selected by the Admiralty was a large clipper of the White Star Line, of 2,400 tons, named after the line, the *White Star*. Women and children were not allowed a passage, but as my husband was in command, and had therefore a cabin to himself, there was no difficulty with regard to me. The troops were on the eve of embarking before it was positively decided that I could go, and my preparations had to be made in three or four days.

On the 5th July, 1860, the *White Star* made fast to the strong Liverpool tug that had towed her from the Mersey, and went down the channel from Gravesend at the rate of six knots an hour. From a distance I saw the last dear spot of English ground, the gay town of Brighton, spreading its miles of terraces at the foot of the Sussex Downs, and I could distinguish, on the hills, the house where I had spent my early years.

The ship was towed to Cork, to embark a large number of recruits. I thought she had been filled at Gravesend, but I heard with astonishment she had little more than half on board.

The rapid change from England to Ireland made me feel as if in a foreign land. I saw little of the beautiful Cove of Cork, or of Queenstown, but what I saw led me to place Ireland, as far as regards England and the Colonies, at an equal distance from the high finish of the one, and from the roughness of the other.

When the embarkation was complete the ship looked like a swarming hive of human beings, and I could not imagine how she afforded accommodation, and stowed food for the long voyage. We lay so close to Queenstown that I could hear the people talk on shore in a brogue I had never heard imitated, fond as people are of imitating Paddy. A beggar woman moved up and down before the ship, waylaying everyone, and screaming in a voice that made us all shiver,

> "Cheer, boys, cheer!—you're going to fight in China,
> Cheer, boys, cheer!—you're going o'er the sea."

This to young soldiers, many of whose hearts were sad within them, leaving for the first time the kindred and the country they might never see again! How many embark for foreign service who then see the last of their native land! Once before my husband had proceeded from this port with the 1st Battalion, and the chaplain had thought it advisable to address to the men a funeral sermon. "Your bones will bleach on a foreign shore, while mine will be gathered to the tomb of my fathers," said the reverend speaker. I cannot say what became of his bones; but the other portion of his prophecy was nearly fulfilled, for those of the gallant men he addressed were scattered over India, and few lived to share in the glory they had gained for their regiment.

Two small Cork steamers towed out the big Australian ship, looking, as she left, more like an Irish fair than an ordinary trooper. It is surprising how soon necessity forces people into their places, and it only needed a few days for even this great body of recruits, now numbering just one thousand men, to assume something of the appearance of an organized regiment.

One of the most difficult tasks that can be entrusted to an officer is that of conveying a very large number of young and undisciplined soldiers to a point at the extreme end of the earth. The mainspring of army discipline is in the non-commissioned officers, and these troops usually proceed to their destination without any, except such as are extemporised for the voyage. Young lads, full of high spirits, unaccustomed to the restraints of discipline, many ill-trained, and some embodying the very essence of wickedness, men much older, who have failed in everything, unchecked by the stern presence of the non-commissioned officers, with whom they dare not trifle, are found a difficult society to deal with.

Under such circumstances it is wise to bring other influences besides the fear of military law to bear upon them, and Colonel M. was highly fortunate in the surgeon-major appointed to the medical charge, as well as in some of the other officers. The task this gentleman set himself and carried out was so remarkable, that it deserves to be recorded. A subscription was made by the officers for the purchase of materials to establish a school, which were procured at Cork. From different societies the Doctor was presented with a trunk-full of tracts and religious books, and the Government always provide a library and a box of amusing games. With these materials the Doctor set to work with unequalled energy to employ the time and thoughts of the men. After half a dozen hours spent between decks, in the evening he assembled all that were willing to attend, and after singing a psalm and offering prayers, he read and expounded the Bible.

I was curious to see if he could maintain this practice in the extreme heat of the tropics. His determination, I saw, was proof against adverse circumstances, but would it be so with his congregation? To my astonishment the attendance remained good to the end, and the effect on some was lasting. The men little knew with what toil this was purchased. To them the clear and animated interpretation appeared to flow without an effort. In reality, all the time not given to them, to meals, or to sleep, was spent in diligent study, that by constant novelty and change he might keep their interest alive.

One day, while in the Bay of Biscay, sea smooth, the air clear and cool, I was on deck enjoying the balmy breeze, and almost expecting to sight the shores of Spain, when suddenly the air grew dark. I looked to see what was obscuring the sun—not a cloud was in the sky. Darker it grew—every face was raised to search for the threatening squall, but no squall came. Alarm was painted on many cheeks that turned ghastly in the strange and fading light. The captain came up from below.

The mate's voice rang out to the men already there, "Stand by the halliards!"

In great perplexity the barometers were consulted, but they gave no explanation, and it was not till an idea flashed on the captain that he turned from the instruments to an almanac, and found the surmise correct. It was a total eclipse of the sun, and many *savans* from England were assembled near the spot expressly to see this sight.

The sea-gulls fluttered aloft in terror and amazement; the fowls, accustomed in their coops to artificial changes, steadied themselves on one leg and nestled to sleep. Though dark, it was not like night—the horizon was tinged all round with a strange light. In one direction this grew more intense, and came on towards us brighter and brighter. I could trace the rays of the sun as they shot over the barrier—a waterfall of beams. I watched for the first returning glimpse of his own majesty, and caught the brilliant ray, little larger than a pin's head, like lightning flashing all at once upon my eye.

The dark shadow retreated like a legion of ghosts over the sea, followed by what took the shape, to my excited fancy, of the angel of light. The cocks began to crow, and there was a joyousness on the faces around, as if we had escaped from some impending danger.

To know how the Melbourne clippers make their surprising passages, it is necessary to sail in one south of the Cape, where the strong westerly gales blow. With every stitch of canvas spread, with the storm howling aloft, our ship tore through the ocean, leaving a broad white line behind as far as I could see. There was no rolling, no pitching. The enormous mass was pressed down and driven on, trembling and quivering as she made her way through the big waves. Floating birds and fields of foam went gleaming by as trees and meadows by the window of a train in motion. Specks could be seen ahead. In two hours we were close to a ship with reefed topsails and topgallant sails, and we passed her as a race-horse passes a broken-down hack.

I could see the spray fall from the bows of the vessel we were leaving behind, as quickly as if she were lying at anchor. I could scarcely believe both of us to be borne along by the same breeze, till I looked at the acres of canvas bending and straining the masts of our ship, Nothing that floats could then have passed the *White Star*, save a faster clipper, propelled in the same manner.

We were in a latitude in the southern hemisphere similar to that of the Mediterranean in the northern, and in less than a week we ran the whole length of that sea from Gibraltar to the Holy Land, averaging each day some three hundred geographical miles.

Australia is only separated from Asia by a chain of islands. When a ship passes between any of these, she changes a boundless and fathomless ocean, agitated by perpetual breezes, for narrow, shallow, rocky, and dangerous seas; cool and fine weather for stifling heat, rain, calms, and currents. The strong south-east trade carried us to the entrance of the strait separating Java from Sumatra. Then the wind left us, and from a swift vigorous ship we became an inert, lifeless log.

Ships are sometimes described as helpless in a storm. My experience goes to prove that there it is they are really noble, "behaving splendidly," as sailors love to say. What can be finer than the way in which a well-built, well-found, strong ship meets any gale except a hurricane? I have looked with amazement at the ponderous mass rising lightly, with the ease of a giant, over an angry wave rushing on crested with foam. Then, indeed, the fond praise of the crew was justified, and the vessel asserted itself to be the noblest work of man. No, it is not in the gale, but in the calm, that a ship becomes a truly helpless and miserable object.

An island was seen ahead as I went below. After an absence of two or three hours I returned to the deck—the island was astern. "So we are going after all," I said to the captain. "Yes," he answered, with a sigh, "going round." The vessel drifting with the current had merely turned her stern to where her bow had pointed. Oh! weary days—oh! weary weeks! Steaming sun—heavy rain—waterspouts rising into or pouring from the sky, and the great black ship drifting with her human freight. No wonder that the hospital was filled, that the men grew desponding, and turned in loathing from their rancid pork.

A singular disease prevailed in the *White Star*, called moon-blindness, and caused much discussion among our medical officers. The number affected was so considerable that it became serious. At first the opinion was that the soldiers were striving to escape watch and guard, and the treatment became very severe. Experience showed that the disease was not feigned, and two or three of those suffering from it had to be led about in the twilight even after landing. Awnings were spread for the men at night, as well as during the day, and the strictest orders were issued against sleeping in the light of the moon.

The first and almost the only death occurred from a sad accident. A rifleman was seated close to the main-mast. He was with a party discussing the question of what they would do on their return home, when the pin of an iron block broke loose, and gathering force in its descent, fell like a bolt from heaven on his head, penetrated to his brain, and stretched him speechless and dying at his comrades' feet. Only two others were buried during this voyage —the longest and the most trying that can be made —and we had therefore much cause for congratulation.

Before commencing the last and worst stage of the passage, from Sunda to Hong-Kong, we paid a visit to Anjer. It is situated in the strait to the north-west of Java, and vessels must go close by it on their way through. The town has all the neatness of a Dutch settlement, and all the beauty of that loveliest of tropical islands—Java. The finest tree I ever saw was here. The foliage commenced not above a score of feet from the ground, and formed a large circle of impenetrable shade around the giant stem. Up in its huge branches I saw a platform, occupying but a small space in the monster tree, though twenty people could dine there with comfort. A ladder led up to the platform, and from it rose high over the tree a staff bearing the flag of Holland. On our way to the shore, we met the barge with the Commandant, attended by an officer and two of our party, on his way to pay us a visit. He had kindly brought off for me a large bouquet of Java flowers.

The officers of our ship who accompanied this party had called at the fort, and found the garrison making merry on the birthday of the Commandant. The hospitable Dutch at once pounced on them, and the Queen's health was proposed and drunk in bumpers. Hands were joined, and the astonished Englishmen in wonder beheld themselves dancing round in a circle, and shouting merrily, with men whose faces they did not know, whose language they did not talk, and whose manners they had always imagined to be heavy and sombre. Two quiet gentlemen passing that way had heard the noise of the saturnalia, and avoided the locality, little dreaming that some of their own brethren were assisting the staid and solid Dutch.

At the excellent hotel we met the captain of a fine American ship that had just arrived from Singapore. "Well, captain," said the Yankee, "I guess you are going to Hong-Kong, and I can tell you the weather you will have. Sir, you will have a solid calm. I have just come from Singapore, and I have been a *solid month*."

This free and enlightened citizen sat in an easy chair in the verandah, with his feet up and his head back, the smoke of a cigar curling from the lips that carried such consternation to our circle. Our worst fears were confirmed.

We were off Saigon, where the French are finding such disastrous employment for their army, before the weary days of calm and rain drew to a close, and we had then sailed half-way round the world in less time than we had taken for the few hundred miles from Sunda to the coast of Cochin China.

Here our slow progress was arrested, and we came to a stop. The north-east monsoon, though a head wind, was eagerly welcomed, and the ship began to move rapidly through the water on a zig-zag course. Pulo Sapeta, or the Shoe Rock, came in sight, and day went by after day, and still we continued moving rapidly to the right and to the left of that horrid rock. At last we got what the sailors call a slant, and stood away without sighting it for two days. The weather was very thick, and the ship had to rely on the dead reckoning. One evening the fog lifted, and showed us the horizon on our front. I could scarcely trust my eyes when the first object they beheld was Pulo Sapeta! We were beating against a current running down the coast at more than two miles an hour. Then the wind, as if weary of balking us, veered a few points. Away went the swift ship, and we reached Hong-Kong on the first day of November.

CHAPTER XIII.

Chinese Junks—A Celestial Pilot—Pigeon English—Approach to Hong-Kong—Its Harbour and Shipping—Doctors' Shops—Sampans—Chinese Females—A Marine Portrait Painter—Cooking—Victoria Peak—Character of Hong-Kong.

THE first I saw of China and the Chinese was a couple of junks slowly sailing close and parallel to each other—they were fishing, with nets over the side. As we neared the land we came on a swarm of junks crossing and re-crossing each other, as they beat to windward, like a fleet of herring-boats from a western bay of Scotland, or from the Isle of Man.

While the ship was running towards the rocky coast, before she penetrated between the island-barrier, a little sailing-boat attracted our attention, with a big flag at her mast-head, which she frantically hauled up and down. Our sails were kept shivering in the wind, as the pilot-boat steered rapidly for us, the long swell pitching her like a cockle-shell as she neared. The tiller, which was in the hands of an old woman, who made way for a man as she came alongside, was handled in a way worthy of a Deal boatman. The pilot, when he stood upon our deck, looked as if he had been thrown there.

We all looked with surprise at the figure that strutted up to the captain with a bundle of papers in his hand, as if he knew himself to be the right man in the right place. His head and feet were bare; the hair was shaven off the front, and fell in a long tail behind; his flat face was unencumbered by a hair; eyes and nose small, mouth large. He was dressed in a loose blue cotton blouse, fitting close to the neck, and without a collar, with full trousers of the same material. The captain unfolded a paper from the bundle, and read,

"This is to certify that Luen-chun, Chinese pilot, took the ship *White Squall* into the harbour of Hong-Kong, and that I consider him a good pilot, and up to his work.

(Signed) "JOHN SMITH, Commander
"Ship *White Squall*."

The captain looked over the bundle, asked a few questions, and the Chinaman took charge. He turned to the mate, ordered the yards to be braced forward, and shouted to the man at the wheel "Luff!" as if he were the owner; while the soldiers gazed with their mouths open, astonished at the idea of being taken into port by one of the men they had been sent from England to kill, and who ordered people about as if he were the captain of a man-of-war.

No sooner was the ship in the right direction, than the pilot was surrounded by officers anxious for news of the war. How to extract intelligence from him was the question.

"Let me speak," said the Doctor, who, for several years, had been quartered in Hong-Kong. "I know the jargon."

"Room for the Doctor," cried the others; and he and the pilot were soon the centre of a circle.

"Now, Johnny, you savez," commenced the Surgeon-Major, in a short quick tone; then he continued, in a measured drawl, "Number one—Mandarin—Peking—throat cut?" with a sharp motion of his finger across his throat.

The Chinaman was proof against every method of putting this question known to the Doctor, who still asserted to his now unbelieving audience his knowledge of "pigeon-English," attributing his failure to the obstinacy and stupidity of the pilot, who had turned on his heel.

The sea-board of the south of China is broken by islands, bays, and indentations; and as the coast is high and barren, such estuaries have proved a retreat and hiding-place for pirates, with whom they swarm. A net-work of these islands spreads out at the mouth of the Canton river, and one ceded to us forms our colony of Hong-Kong. This rugged rock, with a circuit of some sixteen miles, is bold, rising precipitously out of the sea, with deep water around. A vessel coming from the south, after penetrating through a long barrier of islands forming the coast-line, approaches Hong-Kong with the mainland on the left and the colony on the right. The continent circles nearly half-way round the island, and the harbour is the channel between.

Two points from the island mark the boundary; the west at a rock called Green Island—to the east, where it ends below the Lymoon Passage, the entrance for ships approaching from the north. The harbour can therefore be entered from either end, the ship simply placing the colony, with the island barrier, between itself and the open sea.

At the west end the channel is several miles broad. Near the east it is invaded by a promontory projecting from the mainland towards the city, which it approaches to within a nautical mile. Hong-Kong is nearest to the continent in the Lymoon Passage, where it looks more like a deep river than a strait. The tongue which projects into the harbour is called Kowloom. The value of a comparatively level portion of land, running into deep water to within a mile of the colony, was so great that these few thousand acres of barren land became the subject of an article in the Treaty of Tientsin, formally ceding the block to the British Crown.

This harbour has been not inaptly compared to an estuary on the west coast of Scotland, such as Loch Long. The high and abrupt island—green, though dull in colour, with masses of dark granite, having a glazed and shiny look, as if water were falling down the sides—might readily pass for a Scottish mountain. In long lines of white houses the city curves with the coast, and dark and precipitous above towers the Peak of Victoria. Streaks of red shew the course of the roads and the cuttings for buildings, but the mountain slopes look bare, and are wanting in variety of colour; they are certainly without the heather of the Scottish hills. The ranges of the mainland rise to the dignity of mountains, and curving with the island, send lines of spurs down into the harbour, one forming the promontory of Kowloom. The edges of these spurs are bare, and their bald ridges have a singular effect, the hues changing with the light, and with the sky; but they often varied from each other, and even from themselves, light yellow or red generally predominating.

Huge black boulders were dotted all over these spurs, and when the outlines rose to a peak, that peak was crowned with a giant stone. I could trace the vegetation from the top; at first poor, then increasing, till in the hollows here and there it grew into trees, or spread out into the bright green of an elaborate cultivation.

Looking beyond the Kowloom promontory, the ranges of the mainland rose precipitously, and came forward to meet the island, till the whole seemed blended into one behind East Point; and it was only by the vessels emerging from between the dark mountains that I knew there must be a channel. Towards Green Island the view was over a waste of water bounded in the distance by a coast-line of bare and hilly islands. On the whole the scene was grand, much varied in form, and more varied still in colour, from the peculiar power of the sky, that tinted the dull hill-side in sombre or gay hues, according to its mood.

From this barren though striking view, I turned with still greater interest to the shipping that filled the harbour with life. A throng of vessels covered the large expanse of water, and the flag of every nation was unfolded to the breeze. Never before had I seen such a display—not in number, though that was immense, but in variety. Between Kowloom and Hong-Kong, where the shipping commenced nearest the East Point, lay moored one of our old line-of-battle ships, tier rising above tier, and all her stern glittering with large glass windows and projecting verandahs. This was the *Princess Charlotte*, one of the hospital ships, with a massive heavy roof, in reality a floating house.

Close by was a graceful and powerful frigate, a vessel of about 2,700 tons, the largest class of ship employed in these seas. Behind her came the black hull of a corvette, having a streak of red where the frigate had her white painted ports. Black as the corvette, but without the streak, lay a long rakish clipper-looking American frigate, built as if for speed, and not for war.

In strange contrast, an old French 50-gun sailing ship lay close by, her stern rising straight from the water, her bows like the sides a of tub, massive, strong, and immoveable. Anchored near, and also flying the French ensign, was a gigantic screw steamer, filled with soldiers, her open ports crowded with heads, and little boxes of Chinese boats moving round her, passing up their articles for barter on bamboo poles. A heavy dull man-of-war sailing ship came next, with a white flag marked with black, as if a bottle of ink had been upset over it, as some one said. Marryat's code of signals tells me this is the Prussian ensign.

Nearer the shore were two more straw-coloured floating houses, similar to the *Princess Charlotte*; and still further in was a line of gun-boats, with great white numbers painted on their sides, and all shewing our blue ensign. This was the man-of-war's anchorage.

Far out in the harbour the hull of a fine old teak India merchant frigate, built before the memory of man, shews the place allotted to the Peninsular and Oriental Company, and there are anchored many steamers flying the well-known flag, which, from its resemblance to the outside of a letter, has been termed the "envelope flag" by the soldiers, who knew that the mails were carried in vessels bearing the Company's ensign.

From this to the town, and towards Green Island, were hundreds of ships of every class, many of them so marked as to shew they were in Government employ—some infantry, some commissariat, some hospital, and all numbered.

Close to the West Point, quaint specimens of naval architecture swung to four-fluked anchors by hempen cables. These were junks of the largest class, their big hulls dwarfing barques of nearly four or five hundred tons, and their masts, each of a single spar, rising above the cross-trees of the European vessels. They were decorated with bright streamers, which, with the gaudy paint, their queer construction, square at the bow as at the stern, with a giant eye on each side, and enormous rolls of matting hanging to the yards, combined to attract attention. The shore along the Chinese portion of the town for miles was lined with junks, each having on its deck a battery of heavy guns.

Our first view of these armaments conveyed a correct impression of the people. Many of the frowning cannon, mere harmless pieces of painted wood, mingled with others evidently intended for actual service, suggested the idea of these Chinese traits, violence and deceit. From where they ended the line was continued towards the man-of-war anchorage with a variety of steamers and small vessels.

Opposite Dent's lay the *Lymoom*, the new opium clipper introduced by science, her masts and funnels lying back like the ears of a greyhound, looking a picture of grace and speed. Nearer the junks my old friends the American river-boats have a representative, the hurricane deck, the great see-saw, and the house for the man at the wheel, being all reproduced in these Asiatic waters.

The vessels that puzzled me most were two moored close to the shore, having windows, verandahs, and a hall-door, with steps leading to the water. The deck on the top extended the whole length of the vessel, and was covered with an awning, through which passed a light spar for a flag.

I afterwards found that these were called "chops," and were doctors' shops for the use of the shipping in the harbour. The scene became more interesting the more minutely it was inspected. There was a current of smaller craft moving in and out, pressing here and there, nowhere to be seen but in China. A large square-looking box, filled with children, under a tilted roof, was propelled by an old woman with a great oar, working on a single thole-pin, on one side of the stern, not in the middle. A man-of-war's boat, flying its pennant and ensign, came quickly on, but the dame coolly pursued her course, which crossed the bow of the aristocrat of the water; and the latter had to make way, the sailors sending a shower of water over the old woman's box from the blades of their oars as they went by, for this is not done with impunity.

A sampan came next, decked from the bow, with a small space under an awning for passengers, the rowers sitting onthe gunwale, paterfamilias pulling the stroke-oar, his wife the one next it, and the children working those in the bow. The oars were light, and fastened by a ring of twine to a notched upright, so as to be lowered or elevated at pleasure. The stroke was taken with a sharp quick pull outward, the body being thrown back over the water. Once I saw the wife go overboard when the twine that fastened the oar to the upright broke, and she was picked up amid the roars of laughter of her family. The Chinese always laugh at such accidents, even when sufferings and danger are involved.

Skimming quickly over the water, within three points of the wind, a registered junk was observed sailing towards the ship. Its large butterfly-wing-shaped mat sail was stretched by light bamboos radiating from the mast to the end, having a cord attached to the extremity of each, that all might unite in the hand of the man at the stern, who can brace sharply up or let the sheet flow. When she neared us, without a move on board, she went round in her own length, filling on the opposite tack and quickly gathering way. With all our nautical skill we have no boats that work better and easier than these.

The ship was soon surrounded with sampans and invaded by specimens of the natives, the men duplicates of the pilot, and the women with glossy black hair combed back from their faces, and tied in a towering mass, secured by golden skewers, on the top of their heads. They walked without ceremony into the cabins, two of the women penetrating into mine. For the first time I heard the Anglo-Chinese jargon termed "pigeon English." They felt my clothes, examined the brooches on my pincushion, and struck with the beauty of one, took it out and thrust it close to my face, saying, "How much?"

Turning from my possessions, they opened a personal battery, and the first question rather startled me. We often read of places without fully realizing what books tell us. Theoretically I knew the question put was usual in China, yet it took me by surprise when it was abruptly asked. "How old, you?" In their own language they express themselves in a more polite form, "What is your honorable age?"

No sooner had I got rid of these tormentors, than a man with a bundle under his arm insisted upon taking my likeness. He opened a case and produced his card, informing me he was a "Marine Painter" of the highest order, and lived in Queen's

Road. These recommendations he backed by specimens of his art. First he showed me a likeness of a fat woman with wooden legs and arms, eyes fixed and staring, complexion white and red.

Not at all enamoured of his peculiar style in portrait-painting, I turned to his ships and sea pieces, and I gained, after investigating them, some new ideas about vessels, and the way they float on the water.

Finding my cabin no protection, I returned to the deck, and amused myself by watching the people in the boats around.

In other parts of the sea-faring world people go to sea for a living; in China people go to sea to live. All their arrangements are home arrangements, both in large boats and in those so small that it is inconceivable how a family can be domiciled in them. They were scrupulously clean, and their cooking neat and well ordered. I saw a woman preparing the family chow-chow,* and it gave me a pleasant impression of the national skill in the gastronomic art.

Inside a tub were ranged a number of bowls—some with fish, some with pork cut in small square

* Chinese for "food."

pieces, and many with vegetables looking green and fresh to my sea-wearied eye. The substantial portion of the repast, a large pot of rice, was beneath, and the steam came thickly up, cooking the delicacies in the tub. Children that could scarcely walk were toddling along the edge of the boat. They were also to be seen in little bundles at the stern, and an infant's small head was swaying about with the movements of its mother, tied in a cloth across her back.

As we expected, the campaign was at an end; Peking being in the hands of the allies, and the terms of peace arranged. Orders were received to detain the detachments of the regiments on their return from the north, and to forward those of the 31st, 60th, and 67th, who were to occupy Tientsin. This news could scarcely be termed a disappointment, as it had been so clearly foreseen. There was a difficulty in forwarding even the reduced force required, as the steam transports were all engaged in carrying back the troops. Till the means of transport could be arranged the men were landed, and encamped at Kowloom and I became the guest of the Governor and Lady Robinson.

Victoria Peak is the most prominent object in

the island. It rises 1,855 feet, and its highest point is crowned by a little tower, the abode of the "look-out" man. The signal-staff is a little lower down, on the brink of a precipice whose overhanging rocks look as if a push would send them crashing through the houses of the city. A siege gun is placed there to announce the approach of the English mail. I walked up by a zig-zag footpath, and from the top I could see, besides the colony, numerous other islands as bold and barren, and many channels stretching into the coast. On the mainland the walls of the town of Kowloom were visible between hills facing the Lymoom Passage. This is the only town of importance on this portion of the sterile coast. It gives its name to the promontory on which the soldiers were encamped. Their cotton tents were visible in lines, as if the ground where they stood had been white-washed.

On the 16th November we re-embarked in the *White Star*, which was again employed by the Government to convey detachments to the Peiho. She had been thoroughly scraped and cleaned, but the only change I saw was in her side, which now bore in enormous letters "Infantry, No. 22," standing out in white characters on her black hull.

To form a true conception of Hong-Kong, it must be borne in mind that it is a depôt or a factory for the foreign trade of China—not a colony in the right sense of the word—nor a commanding military position. Though it has its governor and council, its bishop, its naval and military establishments, yet it is only a warehousing port for tea, silk, opium, and other staples. It is a commercial emporium on the extensive coast-line of an empire whose government neither could nor would guarantee protection. As that protection was a necessity of trade, it was given by the nation most interested, and Hong-Kong was formed. Except for commerce, the island is the most useless piece of land in the world. When ground is required for the convenience of trade, its value is seen in the high prices paid for small allotments, but otherwise it is valueless.

Our colony of Hong-Kong means, then, our China trading city of Victoria. Beyond that city we have no interest whatever in the colony, and the only interest of Victoria is its trade. The growth of the place has been marvellous.

CHAPTER XIV.

A Collision in the Harbour—Voyage to the Gulf of Peiho —Difficulties of the Navigation—The Anchorage—A Gale—Perils of Disembarkation—Chinese Defences—Metamorphosed English Soldiers—River blocked up by Ice—Ineffectual Attempts to land—Disappointments—The Meatan Islands—Dangers of the Chinese Coast.

OUR first start was a type of what the voyage proved to be—a failure. The Indian Navy war-vessel *Zenobia* was directed to tow us out, but having no idea of the space required for our long vessel to turn in, she had scarcely got her into motion, when we ran straight into the *Red Riding Hood.* The collision detained us two days, and it was not till the 20th that we were again ready for sea, when the *Zenobia* towed us through the Lymoom Passage, and left us well clear of the coast.

The passage we were about to make was considered in China to be no light undertaking at this season of the year, and many expressed their opinion that it was impossible for a sailing ship. The general impression was that the *White Star* could not beat to the north clear of the monsoon, and that, if she succeeded in forcing her way to the Peiho, she would reach the gulf too late to land the troops, for the shore would be found to be frozen in. Perhaps there is no navigation so dreaded by the mariner as that of the China seas. During the winter the wind blows violently from the north-east, the currents flow swiftly along the coast, the rocks are numerous and ill-laid down, the ocean the home of mists, and, at certain times, the cradle and sporting-ground of typhoons.

The shore of the gulf was found to be fifteen miles out of the place mapped in the charts, and the Admiral thought it necessary to anchor a gunboat in front of a dangerous reef discovered by mere accident, though straight in the course of vessels from the Talien-wam Bay to the Peiho. The great length and weight of the ship enabled her to beat through the Bashee Channel against the strong gales that followed one another without ceasing, and we reached the south-west end of Formosa.

The current which runs down the strait, between that island and the mainland, eddies round this extremity, and flows up the coast-line. Hitherto we had been working with the current against us; now we had it in our favour, and our progress was very rapid against the wind. The appearance of the island from the sea on this side was strikingly grand. Mountain rose above mountain till the mighty pile reached a height of ten thousand feet. When the peaks could be seen they were glittering with white. At first I thought this was snow, but a telescope showed it was not. I am unable to say to what the mountains owed their peculiar colour.

We entered the headlands at Talien-wam Bay, as we were uncertain of the locality of the fleet. Nothing could be seen there save the cold and desolate shore; so we stood to the west, steering for the mouth of the Peiho. At intervals, when I awoke that night, I could hear the captain's foot as he paced the deck overhead. The sun had set in a hazy fog, and it was drizzling, and blowing, and dark as night could make it, with the dangerous reef so many had warned us of straight in our path.

The morning broke heavily, and showed us the Encounter Rocks, about three miles from the ship, rising from the sea like the teeth of a saw.

It was late on Saturday when we neared the Peiho, the ship going with great rapidity through the muddy water, which shoaled so gradually that for miles and miles the same cry came from the leadsman in the chains. Sailors say that those accustomed to long sea voyages are nervous on nearing the shore. The captain on this occasion had good reason for feeling ill at ease. Not a light could be seen from the mast-head; the ship was running under top-sails only, nine miles an hour, and the water was but eight fathoms deep. The anchorage at the Peiho is barely within sight of land, and as we had no certainty whether any ships were there, we rounded to, and dropped anchor.

When day came no more was to be seen than at night, the muddy circle being unbroken by a single object. The ship weighed, and stood to the north, where she got entangled among shoals, and was compelled to anchor with barely room to swing.

Next day we tried down the coast, now and then firing a gun, but it was not till the evening that a dull response was heard through the murky atmosphere, and shortly after we made out the masts of a man-of-war, and a few small merchant vessels, near which we anchored. Even then I could not see a sign of land.

A gun-boat, with the Admiral's flag, was observed steaming out, and the smoke rising from the funnel of the *Sphinx* showed that she was getting ready for sea. Colonel M. met the Admiral in that ship, and orders were given for the immediate disembarkation of the men; two hundred of whom, early next morning, were placed on the deck of the *Watchful*, accompanied by my husband.

The water was ebbing, and the time was short for the gun-boat to get over the bar. Several of the officers had, therefore, to leave their baggage behind, to come ashore in the next boat. The day was warm for these wintry regions, and a haze hung over the horizon as I watched the gun-boat till it grew indistinct. Not a breath stirred the stillness of the air. About mid-day a few flaws rippled the sea, and presently a breeze came gently up from the east, which increasing rapidly, the ship was soon straining at her anchor, and plunging over the short quick waves that rushed in towards the land.

Before night, with the yards on the deck, the top-gallant-masts struck, two anchors down, and both cables stretched like a board, the large vessel met the shock of the heaviest gale yet experienced at the Peiho, and I could see on the captain's face the anxiety he felt. Literally that gale introduced the winter. Before, it had been cold by fits and starts, the Peiho had been frozen, and battalions returning from Peking were hurried in haste away; but this was followed by warm weather.

To us the change was magical. The day before had been like one of the last of summer—the day after like one in the bitter regions of the Arctic zone. Wednesday passed without any communication from the shore, but on Thursday the little gun-boat came steaming out, and anchored close to the *White Star*.

From my husband I heard that she had struck on the bar when crossing with the troops, but, fortunately for her, well on the inside. The *Clown*, the only other vessel of the same class, came out, transhipped the men, and landed them at the fort.

Colonel M. and Captain Oliver J. Jones, of H.M.S. *Furious*, on returning to the *Watchful* after the disembarkation, had been met by the gale. The little gun-boat rode it out bravely, with the great breakers roaring in a long line of surf before her, and the tide setting up the river as if all the waters of the gulf were being swept along by the strength of the wind.

As there was no accommodation on board, the cutter of the *Furious*, in charge of a lieutenant, returned to Takoo, accompanied by my husband. A small piece of canvas was set, and the cutter ran madly on, carried by the tide at the rate of full ten miles an hour, and driven by the wind at an equal speed. The waves broke astern and deluged the crew, and the whole coast line glittered white with the roaring surf. Beyond could be dimly discerned the walls of that fort which had proved such a fatal barrier to our ambassador's advance. The only dark spot in the white line was where the sea rolled back the muddy waters of the Peiho. Great bars of iron with sharpened points towards the boat, firmly fixed in the bed, were planted along that entrance. Nothing could have saved a member of the party if the boat had touched one of these creations of

Chinese ingenuity to bar the entrance of the river.

As they were whirled along they saw the junks at the pier burst from their fastenings, and go crashing against the bows of a French steamer anchored in the river, which sank them as they came in collision. The *Clown* had her steam up, and was striving to disengage herself from the dangerous pier near which she was anchored, but she strove in vain. The cutter unshipped the mast, and rounded to under her stern. Ten strong seamen bent to the oars, and strained every muscle to push their boat alongside. The spray flew in showers over the men with an icy coldness painful when it touched the skin; yet not a foot could these ten rowers gain, though out of the full strength of the stream.

The gun-boat let down the end of a rope fastened to a float, and pulled the cutter up by main force. Though the pier, shaking and straining as the tide flowed violently beneath it, was not twenty yards off, no effort of the cutter's crew could succeed in reaching it. It was not till the tide had turned, and the gun-boat had been stranded on the beach, that the Colonel could step on shore.

The pier was still swaying to and fro, as if every moment about to part, while on its rickety planks, with the calmness of a Roman sentinel, stood the solitary figure of an English soldier on duty. No fellow-countryman could have recognised the man. His head was covered with a rough cap of brown fur, coming far over his cheeks and down the back of his neck; his body was enveloped in a long grey over-coat; and his feet were encased in high boots of brown leather.

The country, and even the fort itself, was inundated.

In the morning the *Clown* lay on her side on the bank, with scarcely a foot of water around her, and the *Watchful* was laying out anchors, and using every expedient known to sailors to get her off. Evening came, yet nothing was effected—the gale was gone, the sea was calm, but the day was lost.

Before dawn a sailor aroused my husband, and told him the gun-boat had got up her steam, and was instantly going to sea. The river was blocked with ice, and the *Watchful* rapidly freezing in. Quick as possible he hurried on the few garments in which he had not slept, and ran from the fort. As he passed through the gate the gun-boat was under way, and he could hear a voice through the still cold air, "Hold on, here he comes!" The *Watchful* stopped, the cutter returned, and in a few minutes he was steaming out of the river, with the loose ice crunching under the bows. He was the last individual for the winter that left the shores of the Peiho.

Every effort made to penetrate the ice that blocked up the mouth of the river was ineffectual, and the attempt was renewed further down the coast. The *Furious* and the *White Star* sailed some ten miles along the shore, with the *Watchful* under steam, and two hundred men on her deck. The gun-boat got within a few miles of the land, but her power of forcing her way ceased there, and she had great difficulty in returning through the thickly forming fields of ice around. From the ship towards the beach the sea had a glazed and glossy look where it was freezing. The rigging was coated with white, and the vessel encased in icicles. Where the wave rippled against her bow or her sides the water froze as it fell, and layer upon layer of ice was thus formed, till the mass projected over the sea. Gradually the water around assumed a glossy appearance, and hardened on the surface.

The dark line of ripples away out in the gulf marked the limits within which this process was going on. As yet the ice was soft and easily penetrated, not hard like the frozen surface of a pond. The *Furious* was covered all over with an icy coat, her bows and her paddle-boxes were hung with icicles. The ships were being rapidly frozen in. The air was dry, still, and bracing, but piercingly cold, and the heavens at night had the brilliant clearness of an Arctic sky.

On the 24th December, Captain Jones, having given up all hope of effecting a landing, signalled to the *White Star*, "Prepare for sea." She was directed to cross the gulf to Hope Sound, where the fleet lay with the Admiral.

In these ineffectual attempts to land two soldiers lost limbs from frost bites, and two delicate men sank under the exposure and died. The baggage of the unlucky officers who had been put on shore without an article, was placed in the *Furious*. Months passed before they recovered their property, for the man-of-war became frozen in, and, with the little gun-boat, was drifted about the gulf in great fields of ice. There was a large quantity of regimental stores in the hold of our ship, consisting of supplies for the messes. Notice had been given that arrangements should be made for their transport from Takoo to Tientsin, and the disappointment may readily be imagined when the *White Star* disappeared without making further sign.

My husband had carefully selected, in London, a supply of wine for his battalion, and this was looked forward to as a great treat. It was almost within the grasp of the officers, and their imaginations were complacently picturing foaming glasses of sparkling Moselle, when these were dashed from their lips, and rations of Commissariat rum took the place of the wines of France and of the Rhine. To us the disappointment was still keener, for it was said we were to be transferred, for the winter, to one of Her Majesty's troop ships lying in Hope Sound. As yet I was so thankful that the *contretemps* of our landing had not been completed by our separation, that I did not realize the disagreeables involved in this probability.

It was late on Christmas-day when we anchored among the Miatan Islands, forming the harbour of Hope Sonnd, the most dreary place I remember to have seen except Labrador. The shores of these desolate islands in mid-winter present a truly bleak and barren aspect. Everything is of the colour of dried hay, and cold in appearance beyond the power of description. Though dark, a boat was lowered for the long row to the *Chesapeake*, the frigate flying the pennant of the Admiral, and it was late before the captain and my husband returned from the interview. The gale that proved so fatal to our landing, also shewed Hope Sound to be a most unsafe anchorage. The *Urgent*, to which it was supposed we should be transferred for the weary months of winter, had rolled till the boats at her davits were smashed by the sea. She was under orders for Hong-Kong, to sail next day, and we were directed by the Admiral to return at once to the same port.

Next morning we beat out of the channel in which we had anchored, standing in so close to the mainland that the walled city of Tang-tchou was distinctly visible, with the people moving along the high roads. As we rounded Shang-tung promontory we saw the smoke of the *Urgent*, and as our wind was unfavourable, she quickly passed us, and was lost in the distance. The wind, however, was not long ahead. The monsoon seemed to gather on our rear in mist and storm, and quickly increased to a gale.

For the remainder of that voyage we saw neither sun nor stars. The captain, who had been much tried by the navigation of these dangerous seas, now knew no rest. Driven on by the gale and the current, unable to make an observation, or keep an accurate dead reckoning, he was obliged to feel his way with the deep-sea lead, and to trust to his judgment in hitting off the narrow channel between the mainland and Formosa, and this after running hundreds of miles in a thick fog. No friendly light warns the navigator on the rugged coast of China. By day the ship was hedged in by a bank of fog; by night nothing was visible, save the breakers that glanced from the sea in silver waves of phosphoric light. Any mistake would have been instant destruction. No effort of skill could have averted for five minutes the fate that would have overtaken us if an error had sent us in on the main coast line; and if we did not go far enough, Formosa would have been as sure a grave.

Though our anxiety was great, it was short, for on the morning of the seventh day after leaving Hope Sound, we drew in towards the Lymoom

Passage. As we neared the shore we passed the *Urgent* getting up her steam before entering the harbour. We had left Hope Sound together, and Captain Hire was astonished at seeing a sailing ship enter the port at the same time with his own ship, reputed to be one of the fastest steamers in the navy. He had little idea of the speed of the *White Star* in such weather. Had the captain dared to carry the canvas he would have carried in the open seas, Captain Hire would have found on his arrival that we had been already anchored for twenty-four hours.

CHAPTER XV.

Transport of Troops—Accommodation in Ships selected—Objections to the Admiralty Scheme—Provisions and Liquor—Salt Food—Insufficient Rations for Soldiers on a Voyage—Captains of Transports—Mischief-Makers—Position of a Commanding Officer—The Queen's Regulations—A Dead Lock.

SKIP this chapter you who take no interest in the subject. I think it right to introduce it on the close of our *White Star* voyages, because it embodies the practical knowledge of a much more extensive and varied experience than I can lay any claim to.

England has a greater interest in the transport of troops than all other nations combined, yet she has no organized system. Her means of carriage across the seas is mainly trusted to the mercantile marine. When she wants tonnage, she goes into the market and makes her bargain as any company of merchants. She has, however, a few transports—commissioned ships of the navy—enough to complicate still more the rules that apply to the conveyance of troops on the high seas. The plan has been to charter ships for the transport of soldiers either through the Admiralty or the Indian Government. As the India Office and Somerset House are in no way connected, and act without reference to each other, it follows that two systems have been in force for the provision and accommodation of soldiers proceeding on ocean voyages.

The Indian scale, being applicable only for a long voyage, during which the equator has twice to be crossed, is much more liberal than the other. The plan acted on by the late Honourable East India Company was to contract with the owners for everything, according to an estimate binding the contractors both to quantity and to quality. As the troops had not only the power of finding fault if the owners deviated from the contract, but also of enforcing a just complaint, it was the interest of those who supplied the provisions to charge for a fair quality, and to put that quality on board.

The Admiralty plan has been to provision the

men in accordance with one scale, although the troops, unlike those for whom the India House has acted, may be forwarded to any part of the world. This scale is therefore applicable to long or short voyages—to hot or cold weather. The ship finds the accommodation, the tins, tubs, knives, and the cooking utensils; the Admiralty provides blankets and hammocks, as well as provisions. The Government troopers are of course supplied from the Navy Yards, and issue stores according to the Admiralty Regulations. It is not advisable that there should be two systems of dieting troops. The inferior system is contrasted with the superior, and the men conceive the idea that they are being defrauded. They cannot see why they should be better fed on a voyage to India than on a voyage to China, nor is the explanation to the advantage of the Government they serve.

The main objection to the Admiralty scheme is that it is made universal. The diet that might suit for a voyage of six weeks may not be adapted for one of six months; nor is the quantity sufficient for frozen regions that might be ample for the tropics. A further objection is, that the troops have no control over the provisions. These are given into the charge of the ship, and her owners have to account for the expenditure. For the quality no one is answerable, and it seems to be beyond the contemplation of the naval authorities that the soldiers have even a right to complain. The agents of the Admiralty protested against the provisions put on board the *White Star* being inspected by officers of the army, and an official from Deptford, on his protest being disregarded, declared it to be immaterial whether the military approved or not, as these and these only were the stores they were to get. When by an oversight a regimental Board inspected some meat, of which the men complained, on board one of Her Majesty's troop ships, the presumption of such a course was made the subject of a caution by the senior naval officer at the port at which the ship was about to arrive.

To understand the question, it should be stated that the soldier pays for these provisions not a merely nominal, but a good price; indeed, little short of half his pay. His pay, including liquor money, is one shilling and a penny a day, and from this is taken sixpence for each day's food. As he has the option of taking the extra penny or a ration of rum, the cost without the rum is fivepence. His breakfast consists of tea, or cocoa, and biscuit; for dinner he gets alternately salt pork and pea-soup, or salt beef and plum dough. As the soldier pays, his tastes and requirements have every right to be consulted, and it is too much the habit to treat his complaints as if he had no right to make them. It is wretched to see the men at breakfast, with their pannikins of tea and coarse sugar, of course without milk, and their dry dark weevilly biscuit. They cannot consume the quantity of this biscuit issued to them—to save it is useless, as nothing is given in lieu—and it becomes an incumbrance about the deck, eventually going to the pigs and fowls, or into the sea, in bagfuls, to feed Cape pigeons, albatross, and sharks. Why should they be forced to accept and pay for more of an article than they require?

Nothing can induce the young soldier to drink cocoa. The officials say that it is better than tea, and so it may be; they add that sailors like it, so they may; but this is not the question. The fact is, the soldier will not consume it. There is no use in arguing with him, urging him to take a dose he abhors. He will not; therefore it would be better not to put it on board.

If he cannot consume his allowance of biscuits, and will not consume his cocoa, the common sense deduction is clear enough—strike them out of the scale of dietary, and substitute something else he would like, such as cheese, butter, salt herrings, anything for a relish with the dry biscuit. Thus the taste of the soldier would be consulted, and the Government put to little or no expense.

When liquor is issued in kind, it should be malt, never spirits—nowhere, and never, except on active service in the field, and then only because it is easier to carry. It is objectionable in principle, and not preferred by the soldiers themselves. Under no circumstances except the necessities of field service should Government countenance a habit injurious to the service—the habit of dram-drinking. Nor is it in accordance with the taste of the soldier. It might meet the approval of an old toper, if he did not consider that it was drowned in water; but the great body far prefer a pot of porter or beer. There is something degrading in bringing the men, like horses, to drink at a tub. No restraint should be enforced, nor custom sanctioned, having a degrading tendency, that experience has not found to be necessary.

If malt were issued, it would be easy to give to each man his allowance to drink, like a rational being, at his dinner, letting it be clearly known that it was an offence against military law for the ration to be sold or given to a comrade. On the passage to China not half the recruits took the rum; on the passage home, finding it constantly before them, I doubt if one refused it.

Salt provisions on such a voyage as that from Gravesend to the Peiho, and back to Hong-Kong, just half a year, must be injurious. That they were so the result showed. When, however, the men are kept so long with salt beef to-day and salt pork to-morrow, the meat should be of prime quality. This was far from being the case. When the winter weather of the north of China made the men feel the want of sustenance, they complained bitterly, and it is scarcely credible to what small proportions their salt beef would shrink when boiled. On the messes being inspected, a soldier would stretch out his plate, with a scrap like a piece of mahogany on it, the size of a cake of Windsor soap, and say, that was all the meat he had for the day. It was painful to look at it, and painful to feel how powerless one was to remedy a complaint so just.

Perhaps my readers may be surprised that a lieutenant-colonel in the army, in command of a thousand men, was powerless in a matter so nearly affecting the health, comfort, and even the discipline of these men. Yet the actual fact proved it to be so, as the following circumstance will show. As we were approaching the Gulf of Pecheli, the weather was intensely cold, and it was so evident the supply of meat was insufficient, that the medical officer in charge wrote strongly to the commanding officer, recommending the issue to be increased. On the receipt of this, the officers commanding detachments were assembled, and directed to test the meat, as the soldiers complained of the waste of the salt beef in boiling, and to report the result, with their opinion, for the guidance of the colonel. The committee unanimously considered the supply to be insufficient in such weather, and grounded this opinion on the tests applied to the meat. When the experiment was carefully made, the ration of twelve ounces of salt beef shrank, when boiled and freed from bone, into little more than four ounces. They therefore recommended the quantity to be increased to sixteen ounces, to compensate in some measure for this waste. As the commanding officer concurred in this opinion, he appended to the proceedings his own remarks, and ordered the quantity to be increased to the extent advised.

This order was set aside by the captain of the ship, who refused to allow the increase. Acting for the benefit of a private company, and alarmed by the stringent rules of the Admiral,* for the guidance of captains of transports against the interference of any military officers with the concerns of the ship, one of which he held it to be, this gentleman positively refused to comply, adding that the Admiral had pointed out the course open to the military commander, if he insisted on enforcing his order, viz., by seizing the ship. As the circumstances were not sufficiently serious to warrant so extreme a measure, that course was not adopted. The order was re-called, and the men received, without further complaint, their miserable pittance, as they saw their officers were powerless to help them. Thus the officers of the Crown, acting for the benefit of the trust imposed on them, were overruled by the officer of a

* Sir James Hope, K.C.B.

private company, acting for the benefit of his employers. Thus officers of the nation, in a matter for which they were held to be responsible, were set aside by the master of the ship, to save his owners from any responsibility. Had the ship been seized, the liability of the owners and of the insurers would have ceased, and fallen on the country. The course adopted by the captain, navigating a very large ship in shallow and unknown seas, in a dangerous season of the year, was thus not ill chosen to benefit his employers. Whatever may have influenced his decision in this matter, I must add, in justice to him, that, on all other occasions, he proved himself to be an accommodating and obliging person. It was not the captain's fault, it was the fault of the regulations.

When the ship touched at Anjer, the Surgeon-Major was most anxious to procure some fresh meat and vegetables to benefit the health of the men. A difficulty arose as to the payment, for the captain could not find any clear course laid down for his guidance, though the Queen's Regulations state that the men are to receive fresh meat while in harbour.

From these facts we may learn what the rules for

the guidance of captains of transports are, though it may not have been intended to empower a private gentleman to interfere so directly between a military officer of some rank and experience, and the men over whom he was placed to re-inforce an army in the field, and for whom it was his clear duty to use every available means to land them in good health, and thoroughly effective for the work that might be before them. Where many men are crowded together for a very long voyage no facility for promoting cleanliness and ventilation should be neglected. It is clear, therefore, that the ship is the first point of importance. Some vessels are built of soft porous wood, like the *White Star*—generally North American; others of hard seasoned timber, like the *Eastern Monarch*—generally constructed in England and Scotland. In the former, water should seldom be used, as it soaks into the wood, which remains damp, creating a moist and impure atmosphere, very difficult to get rid of, the sea air being itself so humid. The men associate cleanliness with water, and, unless carefully looked after, will certainly deluge the decks. Indeed, it is no easy matter to keep the wood dry, and the advantage of a ship like the *Eastern Mon-*

arch, or a man-of-war, over such ships as the *White Star*, for the carriage of troops, must be experienced to be fully appreciated. The main deck was lumbered up with horses, limiting the space for exercise—indeed, leaving little more than standing-room for the whole force.

As the ports were very small, the ventilation was not sufficient in the steamy heat from Java to Hong-Kong. The *White Star*, therefore, was not a ship adapted for the transport of so considerable a force. It is advisable, however, to charter big ships, and to send recruits in large bodies to their destination. Big ships are, in every way, more comfortable; large bodies are easier to command. Serious scrapes sometimes occur when young officers are sent in charge of small parties. Recruits are embarked, as I observed in a previous chapter, without non-commissioned officers. Mischief-makers are sure to be found in every detachment, with plenty of idle time, and, as men are more easily led to evil than to good, their tendency will too often be to mischief. Discontent can be easily roused, and the greatest grumbler converted into a ringleader. The recruits, ignorant of military law, are apt, on such occasions, to see how far they can go, and the young officer may be placed in circumstances of great difficulty.

When a number of detachments are grouped together this tendency is lessened, as the influence of a ringleader cannot extend throughout the mass, and the power of combination is decreased. As a rule, when a small party only is sent it should belong to one regiment, and be under an officer of that regiment. When several captains in command of detachments meet in one ship, the senior has as much right to implicit obedience as if he were a general. This is the theory, but in practice it is often violated. A captain of eight years' service may command a captain of sixteen years' service, the date of his last commission being older.

In such a case the obedience would not be hearty, yet it is enforced. If the younger were not a captain, but a field officer, the case would be altered; the rank would be recognised and cheerfully obeyed. As numberless questions arise for the decision of the senior, regarding not only his own men, but those of the other officers, it is advisable that, when a large body is embarked, an officer of a rank superior to the commanders of each detachment should be put on board to command all.

The position of a commanding officer, when soldiers are embarked in a commissioned troopship, is very anomalous. All power is vested in the commander of the ship, whatever may be the relative rank of the two officers. The military officer thus becomes a cipher in relation even to his own men, though still held responsible for them by the Horse Guards. The maintenance of harmony is left to the good sense and gentlemanly bearing of the captain, just enough power remaining with the colonel to make himself disagreeable, and to work as a drag. The regimental commander cannot punish unless power be delegated by the captain; he cannot give leave of absence, place or remove a sentry, increase or diminish a guard, swabbers, or fatigue party, after an appointed hour, or even order a parade—in short, a more absurd position cannot well be imagined.

Is it advisable to place an officer before the men he may for years have commanded in a situation so degrading to his rank, lessening the feelings of respect, and even of awe, with which they had been taught to regard him? As it is of importance not to undermine the authority of military officers, as long as these regulations remain in force, they ought not to embark in such a ship. If the captain is to command, let the officers of companies take their men on board under one of the majors, as a means of communication.

When a lock does occur between the naval and military commanders, the regulations for their guidance will not much help towards removing the difficulty. The impression these regulations give is that their framers were at a loss to lay down rules, and evaded their responsibility as much as possible by dealing in generalities.

The Queen's Regulations are ample for the guidance of military officers in transport ships, but they are not in force in men-of-war, and if they were they could not be carried out by the military, who have no power. The Articles of War state that soldiers, on embarking in a commissioned ship, will submit themselves to the regulations established for the guidance of that ship, and for this necessary purpose will consider themselves under the authority of the naval officer commanding on board. Also, as no military Court Martial can be held in such ship, an offender under the Mutiny Act must be landed or sent to a transport for trial. There is absolutely no regulation that clearly defines the power of the captain over the soldier, and the power that remains to the colonel. In the Navy the impression is that the troops become amenable to the Naval Articles of War.

Though a little knowledge of military law would shew that this cannot be, yet the feeling is so general that there must be some ground for it, in itself shewing the vagueness of the regulations. Soldiers cannot be amenable at the same time to two codes, both repugnant to the law of England. Because they are repugnant, the groundwork of both is that no man can become subject to either, except by his own voluntary act. Troops are on board a man-of-war by no act of their own, and if they are subject to naval law, they may be tried by a naval court-martial for acts which they did not know to be offences. Both in the Army and Navy the Articles of War are constantly read to the men, the military code directing the reading to be once a quarter. No man can, therefore, plead ignorance of the law under which he has voluntarily placed himself.

The following case may illustrate the obscurity of the regulations. A corporal who had committed an offence in harbour, his battalion being on board a commissioned troop-ship, was landed under a pass, signed by the captain of the ship, to be tried by a regimental court-martial. By its sentence he was reduced to the ranks. This was in strict conformity with the Articles of War and the Queen's Regulations, yet the captain, who had not observed the purpose set forth by the pass, declared the court-martial to be illegal, as no man could be so tried without his express sanction and that of the Admiral.

The Admiral had no power to order such a court. The corporal must have been punished by the commander of the battalion, or he could not have been punished at all. Yet the commander of the ship made this course the subject of an official correspondence, declaring it to be a slight to himself and to his chief, and to be illegal. The military commander did not continue the correspondence, and the naval officer had no wish to disturb the harmony by ordering the court-martial to be set aside, and the soldier re-installed in his grade of corporal, although he had no doubt of his power, which was denied altogether by the other. Thus a dead lock was avoided only by a compromise, and by waiving what each considered the right and the law of his service; and under the present regulations it is thus only that the two services can work together. If soldiers cannot be be placed under the Naval Articles of War, except by an express Act of Parliament, the position of the naval officer in command of the troops is an anomalous one—indeed, it may be doubted if he can legally act at all. The law he administers must be the Mutiny Act, while he himself is not subject to it, nor does the act give him the power to administer it.

The question is one full of contradictions. Either the soldier is liable to the Naval Articles of War, after enlisting into the Army, or the naval commander of a troop-ship cannot enforce the Mutiny Act, and, therefore, command Her Majesty's troops at sea; yet, according to the present regulations, individually and collectively, he does command them, under certain restrictions, which only tend to complicate his position if he wishes fully to enforce his authority. If there be any necessity for carrying regulations into a transport-ship, requisite for a fighting man-of-war, the writer, after some experience and thought, has failed to discover it.

At present the regulations work almost as an insult to the military service, at the same time that no object is gained by their use. The soldier, perhaps older, if of higher rank, attends in the train of the sailor, inspecting the quarters of the troops, hears his men found fault with, it may be, confined, and the officers reprimanded. Were the case reversed, and the major to inspect a frigate, directing the post-captain to attend, while the petty officers, quartermasters, and able seamen were censured, the crew remaining nominally under the command of the post-captain, but, in reality, under the major, who knew nothing about them, yet was empowered to interfere in any way the spirit moved him, the Navy would see the absurdity and folly. These ships are built to carry troops, not for fighting. The regulations, therefore, framed for the carriage of soldiers on the high seas, should be in force; not those intended to give strength to a vessel equipped for battle.

The Queen's Regulations on this subject are all that are required, and it is a manifest absurdity that while they are in force in all other ships, they are ignored in her own; and this absurdity becomes greater when these regulations are not supplied by others to meet the case.

When soldiers are placed in Her Majesty's fighting ships, they will cheerfully work under the naval code and naval officers, though they consider the Mutiny Act and Queen's Regulations sufficient for their guidance while in ships set apart for their conveyance.

CHAPTER XVI.

City of Victoria—Government House—Streets and Quays —The Queen's Road—General Hospital—Barracks— Jetty—Temporary Theatre—Chinese Shops and Merchandise—Quaint Sign-boards—Chinese Cruelty—Progress of Victoria—Medley of People and Confusion of Tongues — Buildings and House-rent—Graves — Unhealthiness of the Climate.

Before continuing my narrative, I propose to give a pen-and-ink sketch of the spot where the European trade of China has established its head-quarters.

Victoria, as the loyal subjects of Her Majesty insist on calling every new place, is the city of Hong-Kong; and in speaking of Hong-Kong, as I before observed, Victoria is our only concern, and one well worth the attention of the nation. This city has many peculiar points, as it has not grown like others, but sprung full-blown into the world. With the single exception of Melbourne, it has developed in a shorter period a greater growth than any other city in our empire.

Unlike Melbourne, Victoria had no small beginnings. The trade now transacted in Hong-Kong was created when the island was a wretched fishing-place, where pirates resorted for concealment. This trade required a depôt protected by England, and the protection desired England guaranteed on that rock. The chief of the great China houses established their principal offices on the soil annexed to the British empire, and the exports and the imports, estimated at tens of millions sterling, quickly did the rest. It must not be supposed that all the goods exchanged are stored in the city. It is more like a broker's office, where samples only of the bulky articles are shown; ships proceeding from the harbour to ports along the coast for cargoes.

Were the trade to be transferred to another site, Victoria would disappear as quickly as it has arisen, and the wretched and unhealthy rock would again become a desolate haunt of the pirate. How far the opening of new ports may have the effect of transferring the trade remains to be seen. Canton is doomed, for only the most absurd regulations of the Government of China could have made it the European mart for the commerce of that empire. The opening of the Yang-tse, the true channel of commerce, must have an effect; the results experience only can show. But in the meantime our Chinese city is growing with a vigour that bids fair to make it one of the most considerable of the British empire, and to shed on the nation no small credit throughout the far East.

I commence my sketch, as in duty bound, at Government House. If I exaggerate the pretensions of the abode of the Queen's representative, the fault lies with the Governor and Lady Robinson, whose kindness to me has thrown over the place a rose-coloured tint. The house warm and gay in the occupation of one, may appear dull and cold when occupied by another; then the tints which feeling throws in, may convey a false impression.

I doubt whether there is a Government House in any of our colonies equal to this. It stands on a spur to the left of the principal ravine, across the rocky bed of the torrent. On the right spur is

Head-Quarter House. The architect selected the best spot, had it levelled, and on the plateau raised the structure overhanging the town and overlooking the harbour. It is surrounded by a garden, and the hill falling abruptly on three sides is planted with trees and intersected by walks. The house is therefore isolated, and, as it ought to be, the finest by far among no ignoble competitors. The building is square, rising from a base composed of blocks of cut granite, and facing the harbour and city.

The land at the back, by which the house is approached and entered, is on the level of the first floor, but in front it is much lower, that level being attained by a noble flight of granite steps, a fine verandah running along the full frontage. Two reception rooms, occupying the whole length, and separated by a vestibule, open to this verandah. The vestibule leads to a square in the centre of the house, lighted from the roof by coloured glass—a noble hall, and one worthy of a London club.

Half-way up, a projecting gallery encircles the hall, leading to the bed-rooms. The gallery is reached by a stone staircase, whose winding steps may be seen between pillars of granite. A passage leads from the hall to the entrance at the back. The apartments at the sides and behind the hall are the library, billiard-room, waiting-room, &c. They were all papered and painted, carpeted, and furnished as in England. There was no appearance of India about the place; no stucco work, nothing bare and empty—all was rich, massive, and comfortable. The stables are connected with the residence on one side by a covered way, and the kitchens and other out-houses on the other side, giving the house from the rear a crescent-like appearance. It stands some three hundred feet above the sea, with the town extending before it to the right and left.

The city is built along the shore facing the mainland. Much of its ground is reclaimed from the sea. Wherever I turned I saw evidences of energy and wealth—miles of granite quays and good streets, well paved and macadamized, with rows of thriving young trees. The barracks, hospitals, Government stores, commercial depôts, banking establishments, and shops, are all of a good order of architecture. The most eligible sites are occupied by barracks, navy-yards, ordnance and commissariat stores. But this expanding town will have a fine opening for its increasing commerce on the opposite shore of Kowloon.

The principal street runs parallel with the water, the great depôts lying between it and the pier. Commencing near the Happy Valley, it takes its course towards the West Point. It is called Queen's Road. Why in the extreme East is this street called a road, while in our city, in the extreme West,* such roads are called streets?

The buildings of interest nearest the East Point belong to the leading merchants of China, Messrs. Jardine. They stand isolated from the town, with their shipping anchored in front. Among these is a swift-looking steamer with red funnels. She has just arrived from Calcutta, though few can tell when, for she has been lying concealed in some nook, while the firm has been trading on the commercial news brought by her in anticipation of the English mail. These go-downs are guarded by an armed body, organized and paid by the Company.

After leaving the Happy Valley the road cuts through a hill, passing naval and military establishments, the storekeeper's on the left and the ord-

* Toronto.

nance, the commissariat, and the navy-yard between it and the water on the right.

The General Hospital stands close to the sea, with a battery in its front. The torrent's channel of the chief ravine, with built banks and paved bed, is crossed by a bridge. On the left there is a splendid range of barracks surrounded by trees, the cemented courts being shaded with shrubs. These are the Murray barracks, for the regiment quartered in Hong-Kong. To the right a line of low barracks, rising close on the tide, is occupied by the artillery, and the only building between them and the parade ground is the military prison.

The road then comes out on an open green, consisting of several acres of the most level land in Victoria, of triangular shape, the base being on the sea. Here the Queen's Road crosses another, leading up the ravine by the wall of the barracks, well shaded with trees. It runs by the cathedral on the hill-side overlooking the green, which has been cut at this angle into the hill side. Above the church, and about a hundred feet beneath Government House, this road winds along the hill, parallel with the main street below, passing in its course some very handsome houses.

Queen's Road continues straight across the Parade-ground, the portion between it and the sea being railed off for cricket. On the right a jetty projects into the water called the "Soldiers' Wharf." It is surrounded by row-boats, and, at the junction of the way leading from Queen's Road, the passenger is assailed by little boys and girls, women and men, who point their fingers, and exclaim in chorus, "Want a boat, sir? Number one—have got—have got—can do—can do—captain go—*White Star!*"

At the other end of the cricket-ground a hideous construction of mat disfigures the pretty scene. This is the temporary theatre, built by amateurs and public subscription. To this point the buildings have been principally those of the Government—now really begins the town. From the Parade-ground the street is carried close by the spur, here deeply cut. The houses between it and the harbour are very fine, many belonging to extensive China firms, the block ending with the great commercial house of the Dents. The dry bed of a rocky torrent has been here converted into a covered drain, while the water higher up the hill has been intercepted for public use.

A road leads up the ravine, and is continued down to the wharf, where another pier, the chief one of the city, is literally thronged with boats. The fingers are here more numerous—the exclamations more vociferous. "Want a boat, sir? Have got—have got—can do—can do—captain go —*White Star!*"

As the street progresses towards the China town, it passes the post-office on one side, and the club-house on the other. From the wholesale houses we have entered a region of stores. The shops stretch from the street, an interminable length towards the quay, and are stocked with every imaginable article. But the proprietors condescend to no sum smaller than a dollar—a Mexican dollar—which seems to be the only coin known to the European community of these parts. When we remember that the dollar current in China is worth four shillings and sixpence in England, some idea may be formed of the expense of these shops.

As we move on, the life of the street, constantly increasing, has grown into a perfect hubbub. A medley of strange Chinese shops begin to intermingle with the European stores. Quaint sign-boards with gilt letters on black ground, making still more quaint announcements, hang over the heads of the passers-by, and queer hieroglyphics are mingled with English characters. One informs us that "Old Kip" dwells there; and another, after enumerating the owner's various accomplishments, winds up with the modest statement that he "can do—any mortal thing." A third coolly announces its proprietor to be "Number One," although the numeral on his shop-door declares him to be three hundred and odd.

Enter one of the shops, and if you find the five or six oily-looking men, with clean-shaved heads and long tails, at a table discussing their bowls of "chow-chow," consisting of Chinese vermicelli and pig, you may go out again, for not one will rise, or give any reply to a question, save "no can," "not got." The shops are filled with articles of great beauty and rare workmanship, for in the south the people excel in the carving and working of ivory, silver, and wood.

Some are wholly devoted to fancy articles—fans, carved ivory, and wrought silver; others to silks, shawls, and embroidered work. But many have a joint ownership, one side being devoted to the manufacture and sale of hats, while the other is occupied by native tailors. The chief market is connected with this street by a lane leading to the right; and here comes prominently forward one of the traits of the Chinese—cruelty. A dying fish is splashing in a tub, with a pound cut out of its side, while its companions in misfortune are gasping, breathing the shallow liquid impregnated with its blood, the water being insufficient to keep the fish entirely in their native element.

A great variety of birds are caged in every stage of miserable existence, for all are alive. Strings of pigeons and fowls are hung by their legs, and ducks and geese tied up by their heads; the suffering of the animal being evidently a thought that the Chinese mind is incapable of entertaining. The purchaser, too, goes jauntily home, jerking the poor pigeon along by its feet. The feathers of the birds offer a temptation to Chinese fraud that it would be impossible for these people to resist. Having stuffed the fowl with sand, with particles of which it is also well rubbed, it is then made fast to a scale and sold by weight. Selling by weight is universal in this country, and applies to every article of food. Fish and common fowls are cheap, but turkeys are very dear.

Butchers' shops are numerous, but neither the beef nor mutton is good. Not only is the mutton bad, but it is also enormously dear, a prime quarter costing at least two shillings a pound. The beef is much cheaper and better. Many stalls are filled with vegetables beautifully got up for the market; throughout the empire they are plentiful and cheap. As the street nears the west end it becomes lower in character, grog shops predominating. From open windows come the carousing voices of tipsy people, British soldiers and sailors, I regret to say, taking the most conspicuous place. The houses gradually become scattered. The street, turning by degrees into a good carriage road, rises up the hill, and leads to the fine dock at Aberdeen.

He who has walked the length of Queen's Road some three miles knows Victoria, but he must move up the hill to see its progress. Wherever a ravine cuts down to the sea a street leads up, and each is crossed by others running parallel to Queen's Road, rising over the spurs, and sinking precipitously into the vales. Many of the houses stand where the hill is so steep as to require very extensive building to form a foundation. The material is stone, the whole island being a granite boulder. The enormous rents secured for the houses already built accounted for the vast number in progress, the hammer and chisel of the mason ringing incessantly on the hill-side, and the steep ravines echoing back the noisy work of the blaster. In the character of its houses and the appearance of its streets Hong-Kong is by far the most European town in Asia.

Perhaps no city in the world has a greater medley of people and confusion of tongues. Of course the Chinese predominate, generally clean and respectably dressed; some with their shaved heads shining in the sun, others protected by an umbrella, and often among the poorer classes by a straw hat, with a pike rising from the centre, in the shape of an inverted shield. Coolies with prodigious loads run in the centre of the way, turning the people without ceremony out of their path.

Few women are seen; and as they are of the lowest class, they seldom show that peculiar fashion of China—the stunted foot. When the poor creatures thus deformed toddle along, supported by a stick, their wide trousers gathered by a band at the ancles, displaying the beauty and symmetry of the object for which they have suffered so much, a painful impression is produced. Of all the outrages to humanity this Chinese custom is the most preposterous. Some people file their teeth and blacken them; others tattoo their faces till the features become almost lost; a few extract, root and branch, every hair from cheek and chin.

The West of India has many representatives in the Jewish face and well-known dress of the Parsee. A Hindoo from Bengal, a Malay from the Straits, and the Indian and Persian Mussulman, all are to be seen on this road. Unlike the cities of Hindostan, Englishmen walk here with black hats and black coats, and naval and military officers with uncovered forage caps—a sufficient proof that the sun of Hong-Kong is not the sun of India. In a great group the liberty men of a French man-of-war pass by, filling the air with their voluble talk; and borne along in a string of chairs, from the grog-shop quarter, come the British tars, most of them unable to walk.

Chairs are the ever-ready means of locomotion, stands of them being found at the ends of the streets. Every lady living in Hong-Kong has her own. As the town lies for miles along the water, boats are much used as a means of carriage. The shore conveyance is a great improvement on the palanquin. A cane chair, protected from the sun by a green oil-cloth, is placed between a couple of stout bamboo poles, which two Chinese bearers raise to their shoulders and carry at a rapid pace. They are untiring even up the hills of Victoria, and very sure-footed.

I am not qualified to write about the society of Hong-Kong, as I saw little of it, and cannot therefore know much of the people. By its directing head I was shown, as I have said, the most unmeasured kindness. Even a small portion of that attention with which I, a stranger in a strange place, was favoured by Lady Robinson, would not soon be forgotten, but I have to recall with gratitude the recollection of unbounded hospitality. Government House became to me a home in reserve, to which I could freely go in case of such emergency as might at any time arise in a hostile country to a waif and stray like myself. I knew I was always sure of a hearty welcome.

I think I may venture to say that the best Race

Meeting out of England is held at Hong-Kong. The faulty part is that the expenses are such that no one can compete against the two leading mercantile houses. The horses that run for the principal cups are imported from the English turf, and trained at a vast expense. The scene is the Happy Valley, where, by blasting and levelling, a beautiful course has been formed. The arrangements are conducted with a total disregard to cost, and when the sun shines brightly, and the breeze is cool and refreshing, there are few more gay and animating sights than is annually presented on these three days. The vegetation is green, for the air is ever full of moisture; and the verdant surface, with the abrupt hills rising around, every prominent spot thronged with the holiday people, the stream rippling by the course, and the sea gleaming with the hue of ultramarine, combine to form a bright and pleasing picture. The Chinese assemble in crowds, for they dearly love a sight. The pretty stand thronged with ladies and uniforms, the band playing lively airs, the champagne lunches, and the eager bets, give an air of joyous excitement and exhilaration that justifies the name given to this vale.

But there are few banquets without a skeleton. Look to the front of the Grand Stand, and you see all I have attempted to describe, and far more. Look behind, and the eye wanders over mounds of graves. From the earth that covers the remains of hundreds of soldiers rises a tall column to tell that they belonged to the 59th; and another records how half the crew of one of our frigates found there a final resting-place. I have never been in a climate notoriously unhealthy, where the fact has not been disputed by the inhabitants, and the ground taken is often ungenerous and unfair. The frequent deaths are stated to be the results of dissipation. If so, the reason is that the exhaustion produced by the climate requires a greater stimulant, which re-acts on the constitution, and may degenerate into drunkenness. Still the first cause is the climate. I have heard many doctors discuss this subject, who knew the climate well, but no one ever spoke a word in its favour. Barracks have been built in different parts, in the hope of discovering a salubrious spot, if one really existed on the island. They are now empty and rotting where they stand.

In Hong-Kong men take to their beds and die;

and neither they nor the doctors who attend them can tell what is the matter. There is some great element of life wanting in the atmosphere—what it is I cannot tell. The test applied, however, by the British army is the best that can be given, and blows to the winds all theories of drunkenness and dissipation. The habits of the soldier are everywhere the same. His food, clothing, medical attendance, and accommodation are alike throughout all our possessions, except that they are best where the climate is worst. No one can say that the Government has failed in its obligations to the men in Hong-Kong. Yet the grave-yard in the Happy Valley can tell with what result.

The 58th in New Zealand drank as much as the 59th in Hong-Kong. In the former the men are quartered in wooden sheds, in the latter in splendid barracks. In the former they are exposed, night and day, on sentry without a thought of harm; in the latter they are husbanded with the greatest care, and when exposed, are often supplied with night meals, and with coffee or wine. Yet years on years of New Zealand produce little effect in the battalion; while a few seasons of Hong-Kong sweep out of existence the soldiers that landed with the regiment on its baneful shore. "Look at me!" exclaims a gentleman with the constitution of a horse and the fortune of a prince, who, in the enjoyment of every luxury, has lived in Victoria from its birth, and has as yet escaped with his life, as if his single case were a better test than the experience I have recorded.

CHAPTER XVII.

Annexation of Kowloon—Military Encampment—Hiring a Cook—Force of the Wind—Lawless People in Hong-Kong—Robberies and Assassinations—Catching a Tartar—Fireworks—Waste of Stores—Health of the Soldiers—A Country Recruit—Our Campradon.

When we returned from the North, on the 2nd of January, 1861, the ceded district of Kowloon had become a place of importance. The most interesting question regarding it had not yet been settled—its healthfulness; and the unfortunate recruits came in excellent time to furnish a test. While they were encamped there, the fight between the Services and the Colonial Government could be decided. The best site of the locality had furnished a bone of contention, principally between the military and the Governor of Hong-Kong.

The side of the peninsula facing Green Island and the western entrance runs straight into the harbour like a wall, with deep water. It is to leeward of the prevailing wind, and sheltered in its whole length. Behind it is the safest anchorage in the harbour during the hurricane season. To convert this rocky shore into a line of quays would be no difficult task, when it would become of great value for the increasing commerce of Hong-Kong. A chain of hills rises almost perpendicularly some 200 feet from these rocks, leaving just space sufficient for an old pirate village between them and the sea. On the crest of these cliffs the military had erected some temporary barracks, and as the site was by far the best on the ceded territory, the General held strongly for this spot as the site for the intended barracks. The colony considered the wharves useless without the back country; and certainly these were the lots that would fetch the highest market price, an object of some consideration to Hong-Kong, as all the money would go into the local exchequer.

A wing of the 44th occupied the huts, so we were directed to encamp; and the men's large Indian double-poled tents were pitched on the slope of a hill, facing the north-easterly monsoon. Two of these were allowed to us, and my husband selected a spot on the crest of a ridge, which was excavated, levelled, and plastered; then the two were joined together and pitched on this site. The floor was covered with China matting, the curtains we had brought from England were hung round the side, each tent forming a good large room, which our Indian experience led us to believe would be tolerably comfortable. A few weeks shewed us the value of this Indian experience, in the climate of Hong-Kong. A kitchen of bamboo and mat was erected close by. We hired some Chinese domestics, and unpacked the stores we had procured in England for such an emergency as this.

The first servant I engaged was a cook, who proved to be an impostor. He undertook to supply two others, who, with our soldier servant, were sufficient. The cook spoke a little English, and better Hindustani, as he had been a year in Calcutta. Previous to the new year, beginning on the 10th February, the grand festival of the Chinese, he signified his intention of going away for ten days. He had no idea of asking for leave, he simply stated his determination. I objected, as servants could not easily be procured at Kowloon. My objection had little weight. He laid in the things required by us during his absence, and then, without further discussion, took the leave he required.

Next day I asked for the cook, and was answered by a lad he had employed,

"Gone away, sir."

This boy always called me sir, when he considered any title necessary.

"When will he be back?"

"Perhaps ten days, perhaps more."

"How can we get dinner?"

"Me can do—can do."

"Who? you!"

"Me cook; other man no cook; other man bearer pigeon, savez."

"What! were you the cook, then?"

"Me cook everything; other man pay me five dollars a month."

So our cook, who treated us thus cavalierly, was not a cook, merely hiring a man and giving him half the wages for doing the work he was paid to do. This boy lived with us during our stay in China, and was the best servant I ever had. He was an excellent cook, honest, faithful, and hard-working. In ordering the daily supplies, he invariably asked me "how many man's dinner" he was to get. If alone, he would enumerate two men's soup, two men's potatoes, &c. ; if any one dined with us, "how many Chinaman's dinner me get?" I suppose Chinaman was the nearest approach to gentleman in his mind.

At first I found little regard was paid to my orders in the purchases made, and I was sometimes horrified to find the disproportion between the guests and the food prepared. It would have been laughable, had it not been so annoying, to see a couple of chops supplying the place of a joint, and the dismay depicted in the face of my husband and faintly reflected in that of his guests. I found it vain to remonstrate, so I changed my tone, and made a pathetic appeal, painting the shame a host must feel at not having sufficient food for the entertainment of his friends.

During my residence at Kowloon I was kept in a state of perpetual alarm. The wind was my first and never-ceasing enemy; then came the rain—such rain! One reason of Hong-Kong's unhealthiness is that there is more moisture in a cubic foot of its atmosphere than in a cubic yard elsewhere. The wind whistled round the tent, and blew in the sides, swaying the poles backwards and forwards, as if every moment they would break, and envelop us in the heavy folds of the double fly. I would awake in the night, with the monsoon howling through the ropes, like the sough of the wind in the rigging of a ship, and as they groaned I felt the insecurity of our exposed position.

This dread was half imaginary, half real; but about the rain there was no mistake. When it began it continued incessantly. At first the tents stood it bravely; by degrees, however, they became thoroughly saturated. Then, were the two joined, a stream began to flow into the excavation, and presently, like fishes, we were living in a pond. Fortunately a change was about to take place at Kowloon. The territory had not been formally annexed, and was still under martial law; but at the time that our tent became a duck-pond the military police were abolished, to make way for a civil establishment furnished from Hong-Kong, and we took possession of the hut they vacated.

On the return of Lord Elgin from the north, the ceremony of formally annexing the peninsula was performed. On the day fixed, the 19th January, there was a grand parade, and the union-jack floated from a staff fixed on a hill, which centuries hence will be known as "Mount Elgin," where the proclamation was read, while small guns fired from the shore, and great guns thundered from the ships. As this was before our tent became a duck-pond, his Lordship paid it a visit, and asked many questions about his old friends in Canada.

Our new home was the end hut perched on the cliff I have described, overhanging the sea. The floor was raised about four feet from the ground, on poles forming the framework of the house, the roof and sides being thatched with leaves, and the inside lined with mats. It was divided into two rooms, and well-lighted by framed and glazed windows. The tendency of the wind was to blow us over the cliff, and as I considered the poles much too slight to resist the pressure on the large surface of matting, the wind continued to fill me with as much dread as ever. As my habits were not aquatic, it was no small relief to be raised out of the pond, and I was too thankful for the change to find fault with the hut.

But my chief dread was unconnected with the weather. The most lawless people of our dominions are assembled in Hong-Kong. Nowhere else under our Queen's rule are assassinations so frequent, and robberies so open and audacious. The officers in their little bell tents were weekly the victims of daring burglaries; and that these robberies could be accompanied with violence, was seen immediately on our arrival, the captain of the *White Star* being the subject of the attack.

He was walking after sunset in one of the thoroughfares outside Victora, and had just passed a group of Chinamen, when they sprang upon him, tripped him up, and in a moment he was on his back on the road. A man of great stature and strength, and a sailor, he was saved by his promptness and agility. His walking stick was in his hand, and he was no sooner down than, like a ball, he bounded up and was again on his feet, striking right and left at his cowardly assailants, who found they had caught a Tartar, and ran away.

I had heard that these Chinese concealed themselves on the roadside with knives fastened to long bamboos, with which they stabbed their victims.

The rustle of the wind in the leaves of my tent roused my fears, and my imagination was constantly picturing prowling thieves forcing an entrance into our frail abode. I am confident that it is due to this watchfulness that we escaped being robbed, for our house was the most exposed on the peninsula, and we were among the few that the Chinese did not honour with their unwelcome visits.

For weeks the rain continued to fall in torrents, and the soldiers, who slept on boards placed on trestles, were scarcely raised above the floods flowing through their tents. All their ingenuity was exerted to fix themselves as high from the ground as possible, while the rivulets trickled under them, sometimes swelling into streams. The nights were pitchy dark, heavy mists hanging over the land. Drip, drip, plash, plash, came the rain and the flood in an unceasing sound. An officer placed his clothes on a chair and went to bed. In the morning the floor of his tent, filled with drift sand, showed the course of a freshet. He looked for the chair, but it was gone, and so were his clothes. Supposing they had been taken by a thief, he got up in alarm to examine his tent, and found his shirt entangled in a peg, and half-buried in the earth. They had been swept away by the torrent.

These were the nights of the robberies. On one of the darkest the adjutant awoke. He thought he heard a noise, and as these thefts had quickened his faculties, he took his match-box from under his head and struck a light, determined to ascertain if any one was in the tent. The flash showed him a black form gliding quickly out; he sprang after it, and went headlong over a peg, hurting himself much. On his return he saw the wholesale nature of the operations he had interrupted. Nearly every drawer was gone from his military chest. There was no rummaging among the contents—they took their chance of what they got, and, to make sure, they took everything.

A boat was allowed to the officer commanding at Kowloon—a "pull-away" boat, as it was called—with the usual crew of papa, mamma, and three small children. Every morning at seven o'clock they reported themselves, and earned praise for punctuality in delivering messages, and willingness and civility in performing the work required.

On a fine morning we went nearly half-way round the island, to the dry dock at Aberdeen. After inspecting the *Urgent*, which they were scraping and painting inside the dock, we walked back to the city, about four miles, stopping on the road to make some rough sketches of fine wild Highland scenery. Some ill-looking Chinamen passed with axes in their hands, who would have alarmed me much, had I been fully aware of the dangerous nature of these stragglers. Next morning the newspapers told us that a lieutenant of the *Urgent*, returning to the ship in the middle of the same day, had been set upon, wounded, and robbed. The junks were gaily decorated with flags and streamers. Coloured paper ornamented the poorest huts, hung about trees, and was plastered on doorways. Squibs and crackers were going off in every direction, and the discordant gongs and tum-tums filled up the interval. The noise was incessant. It was the 9th February—the eve of the Chinese New Year.

Next day the roar was like the fusillade of a general action, and the group of junks under our cliff kept it up with great spirit, and I daresay fortified themselves for the endurance of such a noise, by a vast consumption of samchu, the worst and most poisonous of spirits. But my head, which was not so fortified, was distracted by the harsh sounds they kept up for three days and three nights; but the excesses of the first twenty-four hours placed *hors de combat* most of the noisiest. A police boat was anchored before the village below us, and every night the boats gathered in a line about fifty yards from the shore. Regularly as the sun set this line was formed. I suppose it was a police regulation for the security of the place.

The view from the cliff where we were perched was very beautiful. From the windows at the end of the hut, all that side of Hong-Kong on which Victoria is built lay before us. Those to the right, showed us the harbour to the West Point, and away round Green Island, off to the shaggy and distant coast. From the left the view was far up the Lymoon Passage, beyond the East Point. The low land behind the cliff was green with a beautiful cultivation, and over it was a fine sweep of bay, with bright water and glittering white sand. Low hills jutted out at the far end of the bay, assuming the most fantastic shapes, and hiding the town of Kowloon, distant from us about three miles. We saw the first and the last of every vessel entering or leaving the harbour, and the flag-staff on Victoria Peak was straight before us.

On the beach below, to the right, the Commissariat had piled up mountains of stores, patent forage and grain, the oats of England and gram of India. Rice, barley, and beans rose in mounds covered with tarpaulins, some under huge roofs of the dry leaves that formed our thatch, all combining to represent an expenditure of hundreds of thousands of pounds—the waste of war. These piles had been bought at a prodigious cost, and would not now realize the sum paid for their carriage. They were useless to the Government, and rotted where they lay. It is thus the expenditure is incurred—the gigantic sum total, that appears so unaccountable to the uninitiated, who cannot see how the nation has expended so much on the Army, and the soldiers not benefited. The soldiers to a certain extent were benefited, and the officers considerably more so, by the issue of Indian pay. The Indian code of regulations, scarcely intelligible to those who for years had administered them in the country, were incomprehensible to the War-office.

And no wonder—transported, as these regulations were, to a foreign soil, a new state of things, and another currency. The War-office fought vigorously for some time, but as they fought in the dark, they were overwhelmed, and they had the good sense when they found their position untenable, gracefully to surrender. It was not, however, in pay to the military that the great sum was disbursed. Many of the men we took out in the *White Star* were sent back to England in a few weeks. Her trip up to the north, which almost totally failed in its object, cost the Government some eight thousand pounds; yet these were mere items of the smallest account—for war is a series of waste and blunders, commissariat and transport blunders, as well as blunders in the field.

As summer advanced, Colonel M. became very anxious about the health of the men. Hitherto there had not been much sickness, considering the weakly state of the detachments on disembarking from the *White Star*, after the long period of confinement, on salt provisions. People cannot live in such a climate as this in wet tents, with everything wet around them, even when strong and healthy, without injurious effects. Gradually the evil began to show itself in rheumatism, with all the train of diseases induced by such a state of things, and the delicate lads rapidly filled the hospital. It was in vain that ditches were dug around the camp, to lead off the water pouring down the hill; the loose soil was swept into the trenches, and the floods flowed over the barrier and came streaming down in their old courses. The detachments, 31st and 67th regiments, had been sent to the north, and that of the 60th only remained, as it was believed that the battalion of the Rifles would very soon return to England.

Week passed by after week, without any positive intelligence, and as the most deadly period of summer drew nigh, Colonel M. became urgent in his application, either for the men to be housed, despatched to Tientsin, or embarked for England. Before the General could act, a reference was necessary to Peking, and the time glided on in eager anticipation of an answer.

On a clear night Victoria and the harbour presented a brilliant sight from our cliff. Above the black hill the stars twinkled; and below, the lights of the city spread along the base; while the water reflected the lamps of the shipping. The rugged wild mountains glowed with the light of civilization, those of the mainland frowning down in sullen darkness. By day or night the scene depended almost entirely on the atmosphere for its beauty. I have seen the hills of a deep purply violet, the crests of the spurs lit up with the radiance of gold, the water a pure blue, or bright sea green, its edges along the beach tinged with red. The mountain tops rose bold, dark, and rugged, with the sharp and near outline produced by a clear atmosphere. We saw the improvements effected by a civilized and energetic race combined with the rudeness and barrenness of nature, seldom in this world so intimately associated. At such a time the picture was lovely.

I have known Hong-Kong enveloped for weeks in mist; no sky visible over the dull hills, the fog clinging to the mountain sides, the vegetation coming out green, as if mould were spreading over the damp surface, the granite boulders of an inky black, the bald edges of the spurs of a dingy earthy red, as if verdure scouted the idea of such an abode; the leaden sea and the leaden sky completing the dreary, unwholesome, and stagnant scene. Chinese servants, after the obsequious manners of those of Bengal, seem rude, straightforward and off-hand, as if they were what we call blunt, though in reality they are the reverse.

A country recruit, who, by some unaccountable means, was our soldier servant, maintaining his place by mere habit and an amusing simplicity, used to kick and cuff our Coolies and drive the Chinese from the house. The cook defended himself with a stick, and the fray ended in a serious disturbance, which brought them both before the police magistrate. The recruit, who, during the voyage, disclosed his fears to me, had lived for several months in a dread I in vain strove to dissipate of the contact with the ferocious natives his imagination pictured, yet he was no sooner associated with them than he began abusing them in a way that I strove equally in vain at first to stop, the poor Coolies deserting even without asking for their wages. Knowing the man's disposition, I told him he would raise a spirit of revenge that would end disastrously, and so worked on his fears that, as far as he could, he restrained himself. But British soldiers cannot wholly refrain from ill-treating native communities, chiefly because the unfortunate people do not understand what they say.

A strange and well-known comprador brought our market supplies, and was a fund of amusement. He would walk unceremoniously into the house, and with a little nod, accompanied with the salutation, "How d'ye do, Missis," seat himself, take out his spectacles, place them on the end of his nose, peering at me over the rim in a manner so comical, with eyes so twinkling, and a face so genial, that I could scarcely refrain from laughing. Out came his account-book, covered with Chinese hieroglyphics, which, being interpreted, meant "fowls," "Cooly hire," &c., his explanations being accompanied by a voluble stream of "pigeon English."

During the time I was entering in my memorandum book the various items, I would get puzzled with his incessant talk. "Comprador," I would say, "I want rice birds." "Have got plenty good things —me very rich man," &c. "But have you got the rice birds?" "No can—to-day no good—plenty get to-morrow." "Have you the Whampoa beef?" "Not got—very bad beef—Missis no like; spose I bring bad thing—No. 2 thing—no good." "What about the Shanghae mutton?" "All gone—one piecey man give No. 1 dinner—all take." "Well, what have you brought?" "Two piecey fowl—

very fat—very heavy." And heavy they proved to be, well stuffed internally and externally with sand.

An Englishman used to Indian ways is annoyed by the rudeness of the Chinese in elbowing past him in the streets, or pushing across his boat at sea. We had an instance of their cool audacity, even before landing from the *White Star*, when an officer returned from leave late one evening. On getting into the pull-away boat the men said they knew where the *White Star* lay; and rowing into the middle of the harbour, they drew up by the gangway of a long black clipper, where they were paid, and the officer got out. Before reaching the deck he saw their mistake, as he imagined, and turned to the boat, then lying a few yards off. The men laughed at him, and said,

"You give five dollar—*White Star* can do. S'pose you no give, you stay. No ship!—plenty good ship—ha, ha, ha!"

The officer was attacked by a Newfoundland dog on showing his face over the gangway, and the noise brought a surly mate, who treated him insolently. The Chinese, seeing the state of things, began to pull away, and he was obliged to submit to the cheat, paying before he again put a foot into the boat. This was the first trick of many afterwards practised on the new ship-load of barbarians.

Nor did these people confine their operations to mere tricks; they robbed without hesitation, and thought nothing of tossing a tipsy soldier overboard. We soon discovered that a very different class of boatmen ply at night from those who work during the day. Indeed, they are a most dangerous community, robberies and even murders being of frequent occurrence.

In their junks the Chinese have ingenious contrivances for plundering the ship they unload. False decking, with holes for grain to run through—false lining, leaving vacant spaces down to the keel, to pile up with coal; and, when these expedients fail, they do not hesitate neatly to open a package, take out the goods, and fill the vacancy with stones or straw. A regulation to enforce a register met with strenuous opposition, all the lighters striking work in a body. But the Government persisted, and eventually carried their point.

It is strange that there are few, if any, leading merchants or wealthy men among a people so industrious and fond of trade. With a keen sense of the value of a dollar, not many, even under favourable circumstances, accumulate money. In Hong-Kong large sums are earned by labour. The place, too, is cheap to them, though so dear to us; yet the labourers are always in debt. They fritter their money away in marriages, funerals, and other ceremonials, and in gambling, to which every class is much addicted. In observing Asiatic people, I was much impressed with the truth of the old proverb, "Honesty is the best policy." Those most inclined to cheat, and some cannot refrain when they have the opportunity, whatever may be the consequences, were always the poorest and most miserable of the community; while those whose dealings could be trusted, like the Parsees, were a wealthy and respected class.

END OF VOL. I.

CPSIA information can be obtained
at www.ICGtesting.com
Printed in the USA
LVHW040027180422
716440LV00005B/384